THE GLASS BOX

Mark J. Rolli

Other Books by Mark J. Rolli

Time-Out for Behavior (A children's book for positive behavior)

For Jennifer

Thank you for your inspiration, encouragement and support.

You are my eternal happiness in life!

Library of Congress in Publishing Data

Cover Design: Bespoke Book Covers
(www.bespokebookcovers.com)

Editors: Mary Walsh, Jennifer Hurley

CHAPTER 1

The room in front of her was surrounded by glass on all sides, and the door handle was missing, but she had to go in. She had to find out.

Julie stared at the large metal door. Above it, in big, black letters, was a sign that read *RESTRICTED AREA*. She knew working in a confined space with these types of chemicals was a risk, but she was saving lives, so the danger was worth it.

Before entering, she double-checked her blue surgical mask and then pressed her thumb on the fingerprint scanner. The heavy metal door *whooshed* open, and when she crossed the threshold, a warm gust of air shot down on top of her head. As the door closed and locked behind her, she heard the droning sound of machines churning liquids. She observed technicians filling glass tubes with green and red fluids and placing them into plastic test tube racks.

Julie spoke to a young blonde woman standing at a microscope. "Hi, Sarah. How's it going in here?"

"Hi, Julie. I'm about to test some samples with Anaya. Do you need to look at anything?" Sarah asked.

"No, not yet." Julie continued walking around the lab, inspecting different stations, and jotting down notes on her iPad. She continued her conversation with Sarah. "Aaron and I are going out to dinner tonight, at that new Italian place in the city, if you and Ed want to join us."

"That sounds like fun. We've been meaning to try that place. I think it's supposed to snow tonight. What time are you going?"

"Around seven. Does that work?"

"I'll ask Ed, but I think he'll be up for it." Sarah turned to another technician in the lab. "Anaya, can you hand me one of those samples of green liquid from that rack, please?" Sarah pointed to a long metal counter covered with plastic racks of test tubes, microscopes, and Petri dishes.

"Sure," replied Anaya.

Anaya approached the lab counter, picked up a set of forceps, and removed one of the glass tubes from the rack. As she turned to walk back to Sarah, she bumped into a co-worker carrying a test tube filled with red liquid. The unexpected impact caused both lab workers to drop their test tubes. They watched in horror as the glass shattered on the floor, and the liquids merged like water droplets running down a shower door. Lab technicians scurried about searching for something to cover the chemical spill.

Anaya's eyes widened, and she looked over at Sarah, who was frozen in fear.

Sarah snapped out of her daze. "Julie, you have to leave! Now!"

Julie looked on the opposite side of the room at the red decontamination button inside the lab and sprinted towards it. Before she reached halfway across the floor, the fire alarm screeched, and red and white lights bounced off the windows and walls. A locking mechanism clicked by the exit door, and metal grates descended from the ceiling, covering all of the lab windows, except one. There was nothing Julie could do to stop the chain of events from unfolding.

Stunned, Julie looked out of the lab's uncovered window and saw a burly man with a beard standing by a wall with his hand on a larger red button. A sign above that red button read *In Case of Emergency or Loss of Decontamination*. Julie glanced back at Sarah and shook her head in disbelief. *Oh, no*, she mouthed.

Outside of the lab, two men barged through the entrance doors of the work area filled with data analysts, computers, and printers. They sprinted past employees staring into the lab and stopped in front of the single pane of glass.

Julie looked at one of the men, and her eyes welled up. She walked towards him and put the palms of her hands on the glass. He placed the palms of his hands on the glass as well, mirroring hers.

"Julie," he said, with angst in his voice.

Julie removed the mask from her face and wiped the tears from her eyes. "I'm so sorry, Aaron. I tried to stop it in time, but I didn't make it."

"It's ok. I love you." Aaron's eyes brimmed with tears. A look of dread came over his face when he looked past Julie at the technician behind her.

A woman in the back of the lab staggered and fell onto a metal table. She knocked over a microscope, which caused the glass slide to unhinge from the stage clips and smash into pieces on the floor. The ocular eyepiece snapped off and rolled under the table. The woman stood up with her hands on her throat and foam dripping from her mouth. Other lab technicians screamed and backed away.

Julie started to turn her head to see what was happening when Aaron banged on the glass with his fists. "No! Look at me!"

Julie's gaze remained with Aaron's. She moved closer to the window and put her forehead on the glass, then closed her eyes.

The infected woman behind Julie lost her balance and fell to the ground on her back. Her body wriggled like a worm on a hook, while blood oozed from her eyes and dripped onto the floor. She stopped moving, and her arms drifted to the sides of her body, with her thumbs pointed at her thighs.

Sarah stood in the corner, with her body pressed against the wall and her hands over her mouth. She looked through the lab window and saw her husband, Ed, standing next to Aaron. She ran towards him, then stopped and grabbed her throat with her hands.

"Nooo!" Ed cried out. He watched in terror as the same gruesome effects took hold of his wife. Blood dripped from her eyes onto her white lab coat, and her face grimaced as foam bubbled out from under her mask. Sarah spun in circles, then stopped in the middle of the floor with her arms down by her side and her thumbs pointing to her thighs. She fell backward, and her body bounced off the floor with a dull *thud*.

Ed's eyes widened, and he pounded on the glass. "Sarahhh!"

Lab technicians stumbled and grabbed their throats as the chemicals inside of their bodies took over. They collided with one another, spewing white liquid from their masks and blood from their eyes onto the floor. One woman lost her balance and fell into the corner of a metal counter. Her head split open, and blood leaked down the back of her skull onto her lab coat. After several minutes of chaos, the screams of the infected stopped, and all of the lab personnel lay motionless on the floor, except one.

Julie stood in front of the pane of glass, staring at Aaron.

"Everything's going to be ok. We'll get through this," Aaron professed.

Julie shook her head, no.

"Don't do that! Don't you give up!"

"It's fine, my love." Julie pressed two fingers to her lips, kissed them, and touched the glass in front of Arron.

His eyes filled with tears, and his chest heaved with heartache. He pounded on the glass with the palms of his hands in anger. "Damn it! Why can't I get to you inside of this glass box, this death trap?"

Aaron looked at Sarah lying in a puddle of blood on the floor next to other lab technicians. He shifted his eyes to Ed, who was sobbing into the palms of his hands. When Aaron turned back toward Julie, she had moved away from the glass, and white foam was dripping from her mouth.

"No! No! No!" Aaron punched the glass with his fist – *snap*. The bones in his knuckles broke like twigs underfoot in a forest.

Julie put her hands on her throat while her eyes remained locked with Aaron's. She formed a half-smile and mouthed the words *I love you* as foam seeped out from her mouth, down her chin, and onto her lab coat. She reeled side to side and then backed into one of the metal tables, knocking over Petri dishes and test tubes. Glass shattered on the floor, and liquids amalgamated. The blood from her eyes dripped down the side of her face and mixed with the white foam, creating a light pink froth. Julie stopped moving, and her body stood motionless up against the table. Her head tilted toward the ceiling as if she was possessed. Her hands were down by her sides, with her thumbs pointed at her thighs. Her body teetered to the right while her feet remained on the ground.

"Stop! Stop!" Aaron yelled.

The momentum of Julie's upper body continued its path towards the ground. Her shoulders shifted to the right, then her waist, and finally her legs.

Thud!

Julie fell on her side, and her head bounced off the floor with a *crack*. Her body rested up against the legs of a metal table, preventing her from rolling onto her back. Her lifeless eyes stared through the glass window at Aaron.

A tortured cry erupted from Aaron, "Julieee!"

Aaron looked at the man standing by the red button, and without thinking, ran over and punched him in the side of his face. The man fell to his knees and covered his head with both of his arms. Aaron continued his assault, pummeling the man with kicks and punches. The sound of people shrieking could be heard over the wailing of the fire alarm. Aaron felt arms wrap around his upper body and continued kicking the man on the ground.

"Stop! You're going to kill him!" Ed dragged his brother off of the man. "It's not his fault! He was following protocol!"

Aaron stopped his unwarranted beating and shook off Ed's arms. Tears streamed down his face and onto his blue shirt.

"I'm so sorry, man. I am. My wife was in there too." Ed paused, taking time to look into the lab where his wife lay on the ground, covered in blood and foam. His voice began to shake. "There's...nothing we can do now. They're...gone."

Aaron stood motionless, not saying a word. He paced back and forth across the office floor before he spoke. "There's something *I* can do!"

Aaron looked around the room and saw that all of the other employees stood in silence, staring at him. Consumed with rage, Aaron stormed up the stairs, yanked open the exit door, entered the hallway, and slammed the door behind him.

The fire alarm continued to blare overhead while the red and white lights flashed incessantly. A handful of employees were crying, while others moved closer to the glass to get a better look at the carnage in the lab.

"I need to be with my brother," Ed mumbled. "Someone call the uh... I mean, the rest of you should uhm...the chemicals have to be..." Ed's speech slurred, and his words meshed together. He turned his head in different directions, unsure of what to do next.

"Don't worry. I'll take care of everything. Go be with your brother." A woman touched Ed's elbow.

Ed looked at the woman with a pale, blank face. "The chemicals, I...need to know..."

"Of course," the woman replied.

Ed walked up the stairs, stopped on the top step, and turned back to the silenced room. His face brimmed with sadness. "Uhm, the decontamination process..."

"We'll handle it," the woman assured him.

Ed opened the door and crossed into the empty corridor in front of him. After he took several steps down the hallway, he stopped and put his hands on his knees. Tears streamed down his cheeks onto the ceramic tile, and he fell to his knees. He wasn't sure how much time had passed before he took several deep breaths, stood up, wiped his eyes, and continued down the corridor toward Aaron's office.

Ed knocked on the door three times but heard no reply, so he walked into Aaron's office and closed the door behind him. The office looked like it had been ransacked. Papers were strewn all over the desk, and a ceramic lamp was smashed into pieces on the floor. Next to a toppled over chair was a broken computer screen. Behind Aaron's desk, the shelves on the wall that held plaques from his college degrees stood empty.

Aaron sat at his desk with his face buried in his elbow. His sobs were interrupted because of the need to catch his breath. His swollen right hand, covered in blood, was clenched in a fist.

"They killed my wife," Aaron muffled through his arm.

"Mine, too," Ed confirmed.

Aaron looked up with puffy, bloodshot eyes and tears spilling down his cheeks. "Julie was everything to me!"

"I know." Ed swallowed, trying to show empathy for his brother, but his own loss scourged through his mind. "Sarah was all *I* had." He moved closer to Aaron and put his arm around his shoulder.

"We should do something. This isn't the first time someone died in that lab due to outdated, malfunctioning decontamination processes. Management doesn't care about the people who work here, only the money we bring in." Aaron stood up with disdain in his eyes and looked at Ed. "And now, our wives are dead!"

"What can we do? The company is run from the city, and we have no control of the protocol there, or here for that matter."

Aaron walked around to the front of his desk. "I'm not asking you to help if you don't want to, but I have to do *something*."

Ed crossed his arms on his chest. "If it involves anything against the law, we can't do that."

"What does it matter now? Our wives are dead! Have you already forgotten that?" Aaron slammed his desk against the wall, dislodging pictures of his wedding day from their hooks and sending them crashing to the floor.

"Of course, I haven't forgotten. But whatever we do, *won't* bring them back." Ed stood up and turned towards the door. "You're not thinking straight."

"Yes, I am!" Aaron proclaimed. "I have some ideas about what *we* can do. But it will take some time to put together, so I'll be at the lake house. I'd like your help. Can I count on you?"

Ed paced around the office, talking to himself. Images of Sarah lying in a pool of blood flashed through his mind. Anger bubbled up inside of his body, creating a lump in his throat. He interlaced his fingers behind his head and turned toward Aaron. "I'm in."

Aaron walked over and hugged his brother. "You won't regret this. I promise."

"What do you need me to do?"

11

Aaron pointed in the direction of the lab. "For now, I need you to find out what those chemicals were and when you do, create batches of it."

"What about you?" Ed moved towards the door and put his hand on the metal handle.

"I'll let you know." Aaron picked up the chair that he had knocked down and rolled it over to a table in the corner of his office. He took a notepad and pencil from the top of his desk, sat down at the table, and drew a 3-D sketch of a glass box.

CHAPTER 2

Bright streaks of red and orange glistened over the still water as the sun began its low descent below the horizon. A gentle breeze carried the smell of fresh wildflowers past Corey and Isabella as they sat on the beach, digging deep in the warm sand with their feet, touching toes on occasion.

"I'd like to own a house like that someday. On a lake, overlooking the water. Watching the sunset," Corey remarked.

"It is beautiful." Isabella rested the side of her head on Corey's shoulder. "I've only seen a man come out of it once or twice. I wonder if he's married or has any kids."

"Why? Are you interested in him?"

"Very funny. I'm only interested in you." Isabella squeezed Corey's hand.

"I'd like to take you into the city tonight. I have a surprise for you."

"A surprise! What kind of surprise?"

"Well, it's been almost three years since we met." Corey squeezed Isabella's hand. "So I want to do something special for you."

Isabella remembered the first time she had met Corey outside a quaint café in France. He had been sitting at a table by himself, reading the local newspaper.

"Excuse me, is anyone using this chair?" Isabella asked.

"No," the man answered with a smile.

"Do you mind if I take it then?"

"It's all yours."

Isabella grabbed the top of the white, cast iron chair and slid it over to the table where her books and phone were. She removed her backpack from her shoulder, placed it on the ground next to her chair, and sat down with a resigned sigh. After taking a few moments to relax, she opened her biology book and began studying for her final exam.

"Excuse me," a man's voice said.

Isabella looked up from her book; it was the man who had previously given her the chair. She noticed how handsome he was with his short brown hair, worn jeans, and light blue, short-sleeve shirt shaping his muscular build.

"Oh. Hi," Isabella replied.

"Can I get you something from the bakery?"

"That's very nice of you, thank you. I'm all set, though." Isabella smiled.

"No worries." The man turned and walked into the bakery.

After fifteen minutes had passed, Isabella wandered into the bakery for a coffee. While she stood in line, she saw the man with the blue shirt over by a table, laughing with a group of people. When he looked up and caught Isabella staring at him, she snapped her head to the menu board, hung high above the pastry counter. She could see from the corner of her eye that he was coming toward her.

"So, what are you getting?" he asked.

Isabella kept her eyes on the list of items on the menu. "Oh, I don't know. They all look so good. Too many calories, though."

"France is famous for its cafes and pastries, and when they're this good, I wouldn't worry about the calories."

"Sounds like you're a pastry connoisseur. How long have you been in France?"

"Just over three years. How about you? I'm Corey, by the way." He put out his hand for her to shake it.

"Nice to meet you, Corey. I'm Isabella." She shook his hand and smiled. "I've been here just over three years as well."

"I don't mean to be so forward; it's just that you have such a beautiful smile and great dimples. Are they from your mom or dad?"

A feeling of embarrassment came over Isabella. "Thank you. I get my smile from both of my parents, but my dimples are from my dad. He was such a wonderful man." Isabella dipped her head down.

Corey shifted his stance. "I'm so sorry. I didn't know."

Isabella looked up at Corey. "It's ok. He passed away several years ago. He was a very endearing man, and everyone who knew him loved him. He always supported me in everything I did." She paused. "And he loved my mother unconditionally."

"He sounds like a great man," Corey replied.

The line started moving, and Isabella hadn't realized that she was next. The counter girl was shouting at her, "Suivant! Suivant!"

"I think it's your turn." Corey pointed to the girl behind the counter. "Can I buy you a pastry?"

"That's nice of you, but you don't have to do that."

"I don't mind. I'd like to."

"Well, only if you'll share it with me." Isabella was a little shocked at her uncharacteristic boldness.

"Deal."

After Corey paid for Isabella's pastry and two coffees, they walked outside.

"Hmm. It looks like someone took my seat," Corey sighed.

"There's an extra chair at my table. You can sit with me if you want."

"Are you sure? I saw you studying, and I don't want to bother you."

"The company would be nice, and I could use a break," Isabella admitted.

As they walked to the table, Corey asked, "What are you studying?"

"Veterinary medicine. I grew up on a farm in Nebraska with my mom and dad, and I love animals. This is my last year, and then I'll go back to Nebraska for my Masters. What about you?" Isabella took a sip of her coffee.

"It's my last year as well. I'm studying aeronautics engineering. Then I'll head back to California. I've lived there my whole life. Have you ever been?" Corey asked.

"No, but I hear it's beautiful."

"It is, especially in southern California. Nebraska's cold, isn't it?"

"Yes, and we get lots of snow, too," Isabella admitted.

"No snow for me, thanks. I like the sun, the beach, and surfing. I'm guessing you've never surfed. Are there even beaches in Nebraska?" Corey asked.

Isabella laughed. "Actually, yes, there are beaches…but not like in California. Any place with sand and miles of open water is my kind of beach."

Isabella cut into her Mille-Feuille with her fork and took a bite of the flaky pastry filled with rich cream and topped with marbled black-and-white icing.

"How's your pastry?" Corey asked.

"It's delicious. You're supposed to be splitting this with me, you know," Isabella joked.

"I know. Sorry. I ate earlier." Corey took a drink from his coffee and then continued. "What school do you go to?"

"École Nationale Vétérinaire d'Alfort or the National Veterinary School of Alfort. It's just south of Paris."

"Wow. Your French accent is excellent. Mine isn't *that* good," Corey admitted.

"I'm sure it is." Isabella finished her pastry and pushed her plate forward.

"I'm bringing my cup in. Can I take your plate?" Corey asked.

"Sure. Thank you."

While Corey was in the bakery, Isabella noticed that the streetlamps had turned on, and there was a slight chill in the air. She crossed her arms over her chest to keep warm.

When Corey returned, Isabella stood up. "It's getting dark. I should head back. I also want to give my mom a call before it's too late." Isabella gathered her books and put them in her backpack. "Thank you again for the pastry…and the company. I had fun."

"Me too. Good luck with your finals. I'm sure you'll pass with flying colors." Corey paused for a moment and then spoke again. "I usually don't do this, but if it's ok with you, I can give you my number, and maybe we can meet up sometime."

Isabella tried to contain her excitement. "That would be nice. I'd like that."

"Can I borrow your pen and a piece of paper?"

"Sure." Isabella handed Corey her notebook and a pen. She didn't want to appear too eager, so she looked away as he wrote.

"Here you go."

Isabella put her notebook in her backpack. "Have a good night Corey."

"Thanks. You too, Isabella."

Isabella turned and walked off. When she got back to her dorm, she unpacked her books and found a piece of paper sticking out of her notebook. Corey's phone number was written on it, along with a note: *Thank you for making my afternoon exciting. Corey* Isabella, surprised by the message, pressed the paper against her chest.

Now three years later, sitting on a beach in Nebraska, Corey had surprised her again. This time with a special night out.

Corey stood up, took one of Isabella's hands, and led her to the water's edge. The waves broke over their feet, washing off the sand dug up moments ago. Without warning, Corey picked Isabella up over his shoulder and ran into the water. She laughed with excitement and splashed the back of his legs. He laid her down in the crest of the waves, which refreshed her sun-drenched skin.

Isabella put her arms around Corey's neck, pulling him closer, and kissed his soft lips. A wave swept over them like the iconic scene in *From Here to Eternity*. Corey and Isabella lingered in the sand, embracing one another, and watched the glowing sun sink deeper into the horizon.

"We should go," Corey said with hesitation in his voice.

"I suppose." Isabella sighed.

Corey helped Isabella to her feet, and they walked hand-in-hand in silence back to their blanket. As they packed up their belongings, Corey reminded Isabella of his surprise.

"So, I'll pick you up at five, and we can head into the city." Corey paused. "For your surprise, of course."

"Oh. What's my surprise again?" Isabella knew he wouldn't tell her, and although, deep down, she didn't want to know, she hoped he would slip and reveal at least a clue.

Corey moved closer to her, placed his hands on her hips, and pulled her into him. As he looked into her hazel eyes, he felt her heart racing against his bare chest. He tilted his head slightly and moved his lips towards hers.

"I'm not telling you," he whispered, then pulled away and ran down the beach.

Isabella dropped the blanket she was holding and ran after him, grasping at the tails of his flowing shirt. "Tell me!"

Corey slowed down to let her catch up and then fell onto the sand. Isabella tripped over him and landed on top of his legs. She got to her knees and straddled him with one leg on each side of his body. She could feel his chest pounding on her inner thighs. She grabbed his wrists, placed them above his head, leaned in with her face, and put her lips next to his ear.

"What's my surprise?" she whispered.

With cat-like speed, Corey moved his arm down by his side, grabbed Isabella's knee, lifted it over his chest, and flipped her onto her back. The momentum of her body allowed Corey to roll on top of her. Staring down at Isabella, he said, "You're so beautiful."

Isabella blushed. "Thank you."

"But, I'm still not going to tell you." Then, in one motion, Corey jumped off Isabella and ran back in the direction of their belongings.

Isabella laid there, watching his long strides and muscular legs as they left divots in the sand. When she walked back to their blanket, she tapped Corey on the shoulder. "That's him."

"Who?" Corey asked.

"The man from that nice house we saw earlier."

Corey turned his head and watched the man put a box into a white truck and then drive away. "Well, he may have a truck, but *I* have this great car!"

Corey remembered how shocked he had been when Isabella's mother had given him that car.

"Mom. Corey's here," Isabella had called out. She ran to the front door, flung it open, wrapped her arms around Corey's neck, and welcomed him with a warm kiss.

"Talk about a hello,'" Corey remarked, grinning.

"Are those flowers for *me*?" Isabella asked.

"Uhm, no. Sorry. They're for your Mom. They're her favorite, Blackeyed Susans."

"Aww, that was nice of you. She'll love them."

Corey and Isabella walked into the dining room, where, in the center of the table, her mother had placed a large pot roast, garnished with roasted potatoes and vegetables.

"Hi, Corey. Sit anywhere you'd like," her mother said.

"These are for you, Mrs. McCormick." Corey revealed the flowers hidden behind his back.

"Why, thank you, Corey. They're beautiful. Let me put them in some water."

Isabella's mother took the colorful bouquet and walked into the kitchen. She returned with the flowers in a vase and placed them at the end of the dining room table, where her late husband used to sit.

"Can I help with anything?" Corey asked.

"No, thank you, Corey. But before we eat, I want to give you something. Wait here." Isabella's mom left the dining room and went upstairs.

Corey looked at Isabella with questioning eyes, who shrugged her shoulders as if she didn't know anything.

Several minutes later, Isabella's mother returned with a piece of paper and a set of keys.

"I know how much you care about my daughter, and you moved here from California just to be with her. My late husband, God rest his soul, was a wonderful man, and nobody was ever good enough for his little girl...but you are." With a sincere look on her face, she continued. "He would want you to have this." She handed Corey the piece of paper and the keys.

Corey looked at the document and read its contents. His eyes widened. "Wow. I can't take this, Mrs. McCormick. It's too much."

"I...he, won't take no for an answer. You pick up Isabella all the time, and I know your car is having trouble. So it only seems right for you to have it." Isabella's mom walked over to Corey and hugged him.

"Thank you, Mrs. McCormick. I don't know what to say." Corey looked at the keys in his hand and then closed his fingers around them.

"You don't have to say anything. Enjoy it, and be safe. Oh, and one more thing. I registered the car in your name, but the address is here, just in case...maybe..."

"Mom," Isabella interrupted her mother, embarrassed by what her mother was implying.

"I'm not getting any younger, honey." Isabella's mom winked at Corey and walked into the kitchen.

Isabella looked at Corey and smiled. "Now, you can open the *new* car door for me."

A few years had passed since Corey had gotten the car from Isabela's mother, and yet, he was still touched by her generosity. "After all this time, I still can't believe your mom gave me that car. That was so nice of her."

"She loves you like her own son," Isabella replied.

They packed up their belongings and walked back to the car hand in hand.

On the drive home, trees whooshed by resembling a blurry photo taken from a shaky camera. Corey and Isabella sat in comfortable silence, listening to the sound of country music on the radio.

As Corey drove down the dirt road towards Isabella's house, he was still impressed by its immense size. Two-column pillars, one on each side of the front door, guarded the entrance. A wrap-around porch, decorated with two white rocking chairs, faced the direction of the setting sun. A massive bay window overlooked an acre of a well-manicured lawn, while off in the distance was a red barn that housed horses, pigs, and sheep. Surrounding the property was a two-foot deep water-filled trench dug by Isabella's father to make it easier to take care of the farm animals.

Corey put the car in park and walked around to Isabella's side of the car. Before opening her door, he waived to Isabella's mother sitting in a rocking chair on the porch.

"Thank you, my prince," Isabella said and then kissed him. She walked up the porch stairs and sat in the other rocking chair next to her mother.

"See you at five," Corey yelled through the passenger window.

"He's such a nice boy, Isabella. Your dad would have liked him." Her mother sighed.

"Thanks, Mom. I think so too." Isabella stood up and watched Corey drive away. "I have to get ready. He's picking me up at five to take me into the city for a surprise."

"A surprise? What kind of surprise?" her mother asked.

"I don't know. It could be anything. Dinner. Dancing. A show. Ooh, maybe a museum." Isabella walked into the house, letting the screen door slam behind her.

"Isabella!" her mother shouted.

"Sorry, Mom!"

CHAPTER 3

As five o'clock approached, Isabella hurried to finish getting ready for her date with Corey. She wore a white sundress in a delicate yellow and orange floral pattern that hung just below her knees. Some of her long blonde hair was swept up into a clip on the top of her head, allowing the rest of it to drape over her shoulders. She wore comfortable white flat shoes, knowing she would be walking around town.

"How do I look, Mom?" asked Isabella.

"Like a ray of sunshine, honey," her mother replied, smiling.

There was a knock on the front porch door, and Isabella knew it had to be Corey because he was always on time.

"Hi, Corey," Isabella's mom called out from upstairs. "Come on in."

Corey opened the porch door and walked into the house. In front of him was a hallway leading to an outdated kitchen with Formica countertops and yellow striped wallpaper. Just before the kitchen, on the right, was Isabella's mother's bedroom. On his immediate left was a cozy living room filled with a long flowered couch, two matching pillows, a reclining chair, a television, and a brown coffee table.

Isabella's mom came down the stairs and saw Corey standing in the doorway. "She'll be right down."

"Thank you, Mrs. McCormick," he replied.

Isabella walked down the stairs and saw Corey standing in front of the porch door with his back to her. He wore a light blue shirt that hung over his black pleated dress pants. She stared for a moment, admiring how handsome he was.

Corey turned around to see Isabella staring at him. "Wow! You look amazing!"

Isabella's cheeks turned red, flattering her fair complexion. "Thank you."

She reached the bottom of the stairs, placed her hands on his shoulders, and kissed him on the cheek.

Isabella's mom smiled. "Have a great time, you two. Drive safe."

"We will. Thanks, Mom." Corey and Isabella walked out of the house and let the screen door slam against the wooden frame. "Sorry!" Isabella yelled.

Her mother watched the young couple holding hands as they walked to Corey's car. Their young innocence touched her heart because it reminded her of the love she and her late husband had shared.

As Corey drove up the gravel road, Isabella put her arm out of the window, allowing it to fly like a kite in the wind. Corey glanced over at her, and his heart raced, knowing this would be a special night for them. He had been planning this for a long time and was so nervous that he checked his pants pocket every few minutes to make sure *it* was still there.

As they approached the city, Isabella stared in amazement at the enormity of it all. Office buildings appeared to be so close that tenants could pass sugar through the windows to each other and tall enough that you could reach up and create cloud shapes if you stood on them. Isabella didn't go into the city often and would soon discover that this was a special night for her, in more ways than one.

Corey worked in the downtown city area, so he was familiar with navigating through the narrow streets. He drove into the parking garage where he worked, stopped in front of a white horizontal bar, and scanned his badge in front of a gray metal box. After the bar lifted, Corey found a parking spot on street level. He turned off the car's engine, walked around to Isabella's side of the car, and opened her door for her. They walked hand-in-hand out of the garage into the bustling city life.

Men and women, dressed in business suits and dresses, hurried down the sidewalk focused on their own destination. Horns honked, dogs barked, and police officers blew their whistles. Babies in strollers could be heard crying over cart vendors peddling sausages and hot dogs.

Isabella felt her hand being tugged. "We're going this way," Corey said.

They strolled down the sidewalk, passing lively restaurants with outside seating areas where people laughed at jokes and discussed their day as they dined. Isabella noticed a woman dressing one of the mannequins in the display window of an upscale boutique. The plastic, headless body wore a pink summer dress adorned with a pearl necklace and white high heel shoes. The woman caught Isabella's eye, smiled, and gave a modest wave.

Corey and Isabella continued toward their destination when Isabella happened upon the reflection of a man and a woman embracing on the opposite side of the street. The woman's arms were draped over the man's shoulders, and her fingers were interlaced behind his neck. The man's right hand was wrapped around the woman's waist while his other hand was placed in the small of her back as if he was about to dip her. Their lips met and lingered for a few seconds.

Isabella continued staring at the couple, remembering her first kiss with Corey on the last day of college finals several years ago.

"How'd your finals go?" Corey had asked.

Isabella sat up and smiled. "I think I did, ok. The botany final was tough, but I think I passed. How about you?"

"Ok, I guess. We'll know next week when the results are posted." Corey paused. "Want to take a walk?"

Isabella grinned. "That sounds great."

Corey extended his hand out to Isabella. She took it and pulled herself up to her feet. When Corey didn't let go of her hand, her heart raced with excitement, and she interlocked her fingers through his.

"So, what's next after the test results are posted?" asked Corey.

"I'll go home for the summer to help my mom around the farm. Then I'll get ready to start my Master's degree. You?" Isabella asked.

"I'll probably do the same, well, minus the farm work." Corey gave her a playful smile. "My dad has good connections in California and will help me find a job."

They continued to walk in silence until they reached the far end of the campus, where they usually parted. However, this time was different. An undercurrent of excitement vibrated in the air between them, and they lingered, holding hands.

"Can I walk you back to your dorm?" Corey asked.

"I'd like that," Isabella replied.

As they strolled down the cobblestone path, Corey placed his arm around Isabella's shoulder. She, in turn, put her arm around Corey's back, holding on to the plaid shirt hanging over his jeans. They approached a botanical garden, and Corey steered Isabella through the entrance. It was a small maze filled with lush hedges, fragrant rose bushes, carnations, and lilies, in an explosion of vibrant colors. In the center of the maze, surrounding a water fountain, stood several stone statues of children playing.

Corey and Isabella rounded one of the hedges and came to a dead-end where a stone bench stood between two cherry trees. They looked at each other, then sprinted towards it, reaching the seat simultaneously. They laughed, and their hearts raced from more than just the adrenaline of their short sprint.

Isabella put her head on Corey's shoulder and asked, "So, what's next?"

Surprised, Corey replied, "What do you mean? Didn't we already talk about that?"

"I mean with us. What's next with us?"

Corey moved his head around so that he could see Isabella's face. She lifted her head off his shoulder and looked up into his deep blue eyes. Corey placed his hand on the side of her face with his thumb resting on her cheek, leaned in, and touched his lips to hers. Isabella slid her arm around his waist, grabbed the other side of his untucked shirt, and pressed her lips to his with more urgency. Their mouths lingered there for a moment, preserving their first kiss, which seemed to last forever, but was over too soon. At long last, their lips drew apart, and Isabella nestled her cheek into Corey's chest and sighed.

"I can't imagine not seeing you again," Corey sighed.

"We live so far away from each other. Can we make this work?" Isabella asked.

"We can try." Corey rested his chin on top of her head and took one of her hands.

Now, out of college and living in the same state, a few miles apart, they continue to make beautiful memories together.

Isabella felt her hand being tugged. She snapped out of her daydream and noticed the reflection of the couple in the window was gone.

"Are you ok?" Corey asked. "You were staring at that couple for some time."

"Sorry. I was daydreaming."

"We're almost there. It's just around this corner."

"We are? Where are we going?"

"You'll see." When they reached their destination, Corey turned toward Isabella. "We're having dinner at this new Italian restaurant that just opened. I hope you're hungry."

Corey pulled open a tall mahogany door etched deep with swirls and circles. They stepped into a beautiful foyer with a giant sparkling chandelier suspended in the center of the entryway. The ceiling was split into large sections of beveled squares illuminated by dim white lights peeking out from each corner. Shoes echoed across the polished marble floor, and each table, dressed in a thick white tablecloth, was accentuated by a contemporary hanging light. Armless, beige-colored, cushioned chairs surrounded the tables on all four sides. At the back of the restaurant was a long, chest-high cocktail bar, surrounded by a spirited crowd of men and women holding drinks.

Isabella whispered into Corey's ear, "We're eating here? This looks expensive."

"Tonight is a special night. I want to make the most of it with you." Corey kissed the dimple on one of her cheeks.

The maître d', a tall black-haired gentleman sporting a blue pinstripe suit, approached them. "Buonasera. How may I help you?" he asked with an Italian accent.

"I have a reservation for two under Corey Stanton."

The maître d' looked at the reservation list. "Right this way, sir."

Once Corey and Isabella were seated, the maître d' handed them two menus. "Antonio will be your server this evening. Buon Appetito."

"Grazie," Corey replied.

"What should I get?" Isabella asked.

Pleased by her excitement, Corey answered, "Whatever you want."

A pleasant young man dressed in black pants, wearing a black vest over a white tailored shirt and a small black bow tie approached the table. "Good evening. My name is Antonio. How are you both this evening?"

"We're doing very well. Thank you," Corey answered.

"May I get you something to drink?"

Isabella wasn't much of a drinker, but this was a special night for her. "I'll have a glass of Pinot Grigio, please."

"And I'll have the same," Corey remarked.

"I'll be right back." Antonio turned and walked toward the back of the restaurant.

"I had so much fun with you at the beach today. We need to do that more often," Isabella suggested.

"Sure. We can just quit our jobs and hang out at the beach all day. Sounds like a plan." Corey laughed.

"Very funny. We both work a lot and need to do more things together. Don't you think?"

"Maybe we can plan a trip to California sometime, and I can introduce you to my mom. She's dying to meet you."

Isabella smiled. "That would be nice."

Antonio came back and placed their drinks on the table. "Are you all set to order?"

"Yes," Isabella answered. "I'll have the pan-fried salmon, glazed with honey over rice, please."

"And I'll have the balsamic steak with roasted potatoes and peppers, please." Corey handed the menus back to Antonio.

"Excellent choices. I'll put your order in right away." Antonio moved to the next table where a young couple had just been seated.

Isabella reached across the table and took Corey's hand. "You're so sweet to take me here."

"It's my pleasure. I love you and would do anything for you." Corey kissed the back of Isabella's hand.

Isabella liked to people-watch and enjoyed making up stories about how couples had met or who they were. On many occasions, she had played this game with Corey and now was the perfect opportunity to do so.

Corey motioned his head over his shoulder, and before Isabella could say a word, he asked, "What's their story?"

Isabella looked to her left, observed the couple for a minute, and then returned with a narrative. "She's been an artist her whole life but hasn't gotten the break she's been waiting for. He's an art dealer, and she's trying to convince him to display her paintings at a museum. This man could be the start of an illustrious career for her."

"Wow! That's ironic," Corey said.

"Why? What?" Isabella looked at him.

"After dinner, I'm taking you to the museum."

"Really? I can't wait!"

Antonio approached the table with their dinners. He set down a plate in front of Isabella and then put a plate in front of Corey. "Is there anything else I can get you?"

"No, thank you," Isabella said.

"Enjoy your meal." Antonio walked away from the table.

As they ate dinner, Corey tapped his foot on the marble floor while his heart pulsated in his chest. He was eager with anticipation at the thought of his surprise for Isabella. Occasionally he would place his hand over his pants pocket, checking to see if *it* was still there.

"Maybe we can go to California in February and escape all of the snow here," Corey suggested.

"That sounds great. My mom knows a travel agent; maybe she can get us a deal on flights."

Loud voices could be heard from the front of the restaurant.

"As I said, sir, we don't allow baseball hats to be worn in this restaurant. I'll ask you once more, please leave!" the maître d' shouted.

"Can you see what's happening?" Isabella asked Corey.

"Looks like some guy is trying to get into the restaurant." Corey stood up to get a better view. "He's got something in his hands too. Maybe a box or a package. I don't know."

"You're going to regret this!" a man's voice shouted.

"He just left." Corey sat back down in his chair.

"That was odd. I mean, who wears a baseball hat into a restaurant anyway? That's so rude. I hope he's not outside when we leave." Isabella commented.

"We'll be fine," Corey assured her.

Corey and Isabella sat in comfortable silence for the remainder of their meal.

Antonio returned to the table. "How was everything?"

"Excellent. Thank you," Isabella answered. "Is everything ok at the front desk?"

"Yes. Security showed up just in time to escort the man out." Antonio picked up the dinner plates as he talked. "I apologize for that interruption. I hope it didn't ruin your dining experience."

"No. Not at all," Corey responded.

"Any room for dessert or coffee?" Antonio asked.

"No room for dessert for me." Corey squirmed in his seat.

"Me either," Isabella said.

"Very well, then." Antonio placed a leather bi-fold binder on the edge of the table. "No rush. Thank you, and enjoy the rest of your evening."

Corey picked up the binder, opened it, and shook his head.

"What?" Isabella asked.

"Uhm, maybe we should have eaten at that hot dog place at the corner."

"You're such a jerk," Isabella joked.

Corey put cash inside the bi-fold, closed it, and placed it in the middle of the table. He rose to his feet, walked over to Isabella's chair, and pulled it out for her.

Isabella put her arms around Corey's neck and gave him a gentle kiss. "How far away is the museum?"

"Not far. A few minutes." Corey smiled, took Isabella's hand, and they crossed the lobby towards the exit. When he opened the door for her, the fresh night air wafted past them, calming Corey's nerves.

Corey and Isabella walked down the street, passing elegant boutiques and lively restaurants. They turned a corner, and there it was – an impressive five-story limestone building guarded by four towering statues depicting mythological deities. Parents could be seen taking pictures of their children climbing on the feet of the Greek Gods.

Guarding the right side of the museum entrance was Zeus, the God of Thunder. He stood tall with long strands of carved hair and a full rugged beard. A lightning bolt in his right hand pointed down at three boys staring up at his colossal frame. His chiseled face and angry eyes portrayed a fierce demeanor. His arms brimmed with power and strength, while his thighs, cut deep with lines, revealed muscular quadriceps and calves.

Standing behind Zeus was his wife, Hera. Her face was smooth and kind. A tiara on top of her head accentuated her long flowing hair, which draped down her naked back. Long vertical lines were etched in her dress, giving the impression that it was blowing in the wind. Her right hand rested on Zeus' shoulder, acknowledging his sovereignty.

Opposite Zeus, guarding the left side of the museum entrance, was one of his brothers, Hades, God of the Underworld. A helmet called the Helm of Darkness, also known as the *Cap of Invisibility*, sat on top of his head. His face was etched deep with scars from battles in the Underworld. His robe, draped over one shoulder, revealed his defined abdominal muscles. A two-pronged staff, the height of the museum, stood tall in his left hand, and sitting next to Hades was his three-headed dog, Cerberus, rearing its canine fangs at Zeus.

Behind Hades stood his other brother, Poseidon, God of the Sea. A pointed crown atop his head covered hair, as thick as hemp rope, hanging down his back. His curly beard dangled across his rippled chest, and in his left hand, held high above his head, was his magical trident staff. In his right hand were the reins of his chariot driven by two hippocampuses engulfed by the crest of a wave entangled with sea serpents and fish.

Corey and Isabella walked between the intimidating statues and through the rotating front door of the museum. They were greeted by a skeleton of a T-Rex hanging from the ceiling. Its jaw showcased razor-sharp teeth glaring down at visitors. A young man dressed in a safari uniform walked over and handed a pamphlet to Corey.

41

"Hi. My name is Jacob. Welcome to the Museum of Nebraska Art. Sculptures and historical art are located on the ground floor. Paintings are on the second. Crafts and ancient artifacts are on the third. And on the top floor is performance and sand art. If you have any questions or need directions, there is an information booth located on each floor." Jacob pointed to the center of the first floor.

"Thank you, Jacob," Isabella gushed.

"You're welcome. Enjoy your evening." Jacob moved past them to a family of four entering the museum.

"I don't need to ask which floor we're going to, do I?" Corey teased.

"Uhm, nope. Second floor, please."

"We can take the stairs over there." Corey pointed to the right.

As they walked past large metal sculptures of airplanes, Isabella noticed that each exhibit had a pedestal holding a small electronic tablet on it. She stopped at one specific plane and read the information on the screen aloud. "Wright Flyer Designed by Wilbur and Orville Wright. First flown at Kill Devil Hills, south of Kitty Hawk, North Carolina, on December 7, 1903."

"Aeronautics has come a long way since then," Corey remarked.

"It still amazes me how planes can be so heavy and fly miles up in the air without falling," Isabella mused.

"Well, when a plane flies horizontally at a steady speed, lift from the wings balance the plane's weight, and the thrust balances the drag. This creates a lift force, greater than the plane's weight, which powers the plane higher into the sky," Corey explained.

Isabella looked at Corey. "Good to know."

When they reached the stairs to the second floor, Isabella was too eager to wait, so she ran up them. "Race ya?" she teased after a three-step lead.

Corey sprinted up the stairs, almost passing her, but instead, let her reach the top step first. Pretending to be out of breath, he leaned over and put his hands on his knees. "You beat me," he said, heaving. He waited for some sarcastic comment from Isabella, and when he didn't get one, he looked up to see if she was ok.

Isabella was standing still, awestruck. The light from the moon emanated through a large window and cast a shadow on the wall next to her. Her hair swayed across her back, and her face looked angelic. She was mesmerized at the showcase of paintings in front of her. Corey stood for a moment, admiring her beauty, wanting to remember this moment forever. He slid his hand over his jeans pocket, but he wasn't nervous anymore.

Corey touched her elbow. "Are you ok?"

She jumped, then turned her head towards him. "This collection is amazing! Over there is van Gogh. And there, Picasso. And across the room, Andy Warhol. We need to stop by every one of them." Her excitement was contagious.

Corey admired Isabella's passion for paintings. "Take your time. We're in no rush. Tell me all about them."

"Not sure if you know, but these aren't the real paintings. They're replicas. The originals are too expensive to be out in the open like this," Isabella explained with confidence. "This one is called *Water Lilies* by Monet. He created over 250 paintings of his flower garden at his home in Giverny, France, and this is one of them. Many of his works were painted while he suffered from cataracts, and most of them were finished during the last thirty years of his life."

Isabella grew more excited as they moved along the ensemble cast of artists.

"This one I'm sure you've seen, *The Starry Night* by Vincent van Gogh. It was painted in June of 1889 and showed the view from the east-facing window of his asylum room at Saint-Rémy-de-Provence, just before sunrise. He added the village." Isabella pointed to the black shape in the picture.

Approaching the next painting, Isabella stopped and stared. She was entranced by its color, soft tone, and beauty of the subject. Other patrons were admiring the same canvas. Without shifting her gaze, Isabella whispered, "There it is. The most famous painting in the world, the *Mona Lisa*. It was painted in the early 1500s by Leonardo da Vinci and has hung in the Louvre since 1797." Isabella paused for a moment. "It was presumed to be a portrait of Lisa Gherardini, the wife of Francesco del Giocondo. I believe the original has an insurance value of hundreds of millions of dollars."

"I heard the painting was stolen from the Louvre. Is that true?" an older woman asked.

With complete assuredness, Isabella turned to the lady and said, "In fact, it was. On August 21, 1911, a French poet named Guillaume Apollinaire was arrested and imprisoned. Apollinaire implicated his friend Pablo Picasso as well, and they were both questioned and exonerated. The real culprit was Vincenzo Peruggia. He had helped construct the painting's glass case and also worked at the Louvre. He stole the painting, tucked it under his coat, hid in a broom closet until the museum closed, and then walked out with it."

The woman gasped. "Was he ever caught?"

Isabella turned her head back to the painting. "Yes. After two years of hiding it, Mr. Peruggia attempted to sell it to the Uffizi Gallery in Florence, Italy. He got caught, but the painting was exhibited in the gallery for over two weeks. On January 4, 1914, it was returned to the Louvre, and Mr. Peruggia served six months in prison, but was hailed for his patriotism in Italy."

Corey asked a question of his own, "Was anything else done to this painting?"

Isabella turned to him, smiled, and reached for his hand. "As a matter of fact, on December 30, 1956, a rock was thrown at the painting, shattering its glass case and dislodging a speck of pigment near the left elbow. Since then, it's been encased in bulletproof glass."

The woman who spoke earlier touched Isabella's shoulder. "Thank you, dear. You're quite knowledgeable. Are you an artist?"

"Oh, no. I'm just a small-time painter," Isabella admitted.

Corey interjected, "I've seen her work—she's fantastic! She should sell some of them."

"Oh, dear, you should. You only live once, and you have nothing to lose." The woman smiled and walked away.

Isabella turned to Corey and hit his arm. "Why did you say that?"

"Well, it's true. You're outstanding." Corey squeezed her hand. "Want to keep looking at more paintings?"

"What do you want to see?" Isabella asked. "It's been all about me since we got here."

"That's ok. I don't mind. You've never been here. You should enjoy it."

"Ok, just a few more, and then we'll go see what you want."

Corey rolled his eyes. "Fine. If we have to."

As they continued admiring another painting, someone bumped into Corey and kept walking. Corey turned his head and saw a man wearing a gray baseball cap, a black coat, jeans, and sneakers carrying a square cardboard box in both of his hands.

"That looks like the guy from the restaurant," Corey muttered to himself.

CHAPTER 4

Corey watched as the man placed the box in the middle of the museum floor and then reach into his coat pocket. The man stood there for a few seconds, pulled the brim of his baseball cap down to the tip of his nose, and then walked off. He bumped into patrons as he headed towards the exit at the other end of the floor.

Isabella tugged at Corey's arm. "What did you say?" She turned her head in the direction Corey was staring. "What are you looking at?"

"Did you see that guy? He bumped into me and then put that box down over there." Corey pointed to the middle of the gallery floor.

"What's in it?" Isabella asked.

"I don't know. We should tell security, though. It could be dangerous."

Corey and Isabella walked towards the stairs, and when they reached the top step going down, they heard a scream and looked back towards the middle of the museum floor. Several feet from the box, they saw a man on his knees with both of his hands around his throat. He appeared to be having difficulty breathing.

A woman next to the man cried out, "Help! Is there a doctor?"

Another woman ran over, kneeled next to the man, placed her hand on his shoulder, and spoke to him.

The man nodded and then swayed side to side as white foam bubbled out of his mouth. Still holding his throat with both hands, he collapsed onto his back, and his legs kicked out from under him. He wriggled and squirmed on the polished floor as if he were having an epileptic seizure. Blood ran from the corners of his eyes down past the tops of his ears. His head thrashed and banged against the marble floor as blood pooled under it, creating a dull squelchy noise, like wipers hitting the edge of the windshield during a heavy rainstorm. The palms of his hands were faced down, while his thumbs pointed to his thighs.

Isabella couldn't watch and buried her head into Corey's chest. He wrapped his arms around her but couldn't take his eyes off what was happening to the man.

The woman, who had attended to the man, jolted upright and grabbed her throat with both of her hands. White foam filled her mouth, and she rocked back and forth. Blood from her eyes trickled down her cheeks to the corners of her mouth and continued over her chin, onto the back of her hands. She swung her arms down by the sides of her body with her thumbs pointing to her thighs. She stood there motionless, but only for a moment.

Isabella pressed her head deeper into Corey's chest and covered her ears with her hands. She heard a *thud* and opened her eyes to see that the woman had fallen to the floor. Isabella looked back at the man on the ground. He was lifeless and lying in a puddle of blood. His eyes had stopped bleeding, but foam residue continued to drip from the corners of his mouth.

Panic struck the second floor of the museum. People screamed and ran like rats in a maze toward the stairs. Museum guards moved into position, directing people to the exits.

"We need to go!" Corey blurted.

Corey took Isabella's hand, and they ran down the stairs. They stopped at the bottom when they spotted a similar ominous-looking cardboard box in the middle of the first floor.

Several people had already succumbed to the same gruesome fate as the man and woman on the second floor. Blood was smeared across the tile, creating a different type of abstract art for patrons to look at. Anguished screams could be heard from every level of the building. Parents carrying their children tried to force their way through the crowd to the exit doors. Sirens blared outside, and red and blue police car lights flashed in circles on the inside ceiling of the museum. Cars could be heard crashing into one another.

Corey looked back up the stairs and noticed that a woman had fallen. She was being trampled by the panicking crowd who were forcing their way down. Corey heard the crunch of her bones breaking like the sound of ice cracking in a pond.

As Corey and Isabella stood watching the chaos, a man fell in between their clasped hands. Corey looked back at Isabella, but she was gone. He yelled her name several times but heard no response. Something grabbed his ankle, and he shook his foot to get it off. As his eyes darted around the sea of people, looking for Isabella, something touched his ankle again. He looked down and saw that Isabella was under the stairs. Corey forced his way down the steps towards her and grabbed her hand. "Let's go!"

Screams of hysteria echoed around them while feet sloshed through the blood and foam on the floor. Men, women, and children, running in fear, lost their footing on the wet ground and fell into one another.

Isabella noticed that anyone who had gotten sick fell over in the same way; on their back, with their palms flat and their thumbs pointing towards their thighs. Her veterinary experience suggested that whatever was in the boxes could be causing a nervous system failure resulting in advanced rigor mortis. She tugged on Corey's shirt, trying to get his attention.

"Over there! There's a door!" Isabella pointed under the stairs.

They pushed their way past oncoming human traffic, and when they reached the door, they found that it was locked. Corey kicked the handle, hoping it would snap off, but it didn't. He looked around and saw a fire extinguisher hanging on the wall by the *Wright Brothers* plane.

"Stay here! Don't move! I'll be right back!" he insisted.

Isabella nodded in agreement and grabbed the door handle, bracing herself as men and women brushed past her. She saw a man collapse on the stairs while holding his throat. An infected woman fell over him and tumbled down into the crowd of people

When Corey got back, he slammed the bottom of the fire extinguisher down on the door handle - *clang*. After his fourth attempt, the handle snapped off. He dropped the tank, kicked the door open, grabbed Isabella's hand, and they ran through the opening, letting the spring-loaded door slam shut behind them. They were outside, and the feeling of being trapped inside a coffin subsided.

"Are you ok?" Corey asked.

"I'm so scared. What are we going to do?" Isabella started to hyperventilate.

"We'll be ok. I promise," Corey assured her. "Whatever it is, seems to be spreading from those boxes. We need to keep moving."

Corey and Isabella looked around at the mayhem that had just taken over the city. Sirens from police cars, fire trucks, and ambulances wailed as they littered the streets. Mothers and fathers holding the hands of their children ran in all different directions. Smoke billowed into the sky from vehicles that had crashed.

Corey spotted a police officer and walked over to him. "Excuse me, officer. What's going on?"

"Move along, please. Follow the crowd to that police officer on the corner, and he'll direct you to a safe area outside of the city." The policeman put his whistle in his mouth, blew it, and continued directing the traffic of people.

While Corey was talking to the policeman, Isabella witnessed a man clenching his throat with both of his hands. Blood dripped from his eyes, down his face, and onto the lapel of his blue pin-striped suit. The man swayed from side to side and then fell onto a table, shattering the glass that covered the top of it. Isabella stared at the blood on the ground, seeping out from under the man's face. Her stomach churned, and she turned back toward Corey.

Corey saw an alley across the street. "Over there!"

He gripped Isabella's hand tighter, and they forced their way through the labyrinth of people toward the alley. Upon reaching it, they looked back at the bedlam behind them.

The sidewalk in front of the museum was littered with dead bodies. Children sobbed in their parents' arms while police officers struggled to maintain order in the streets, which seemed impossible in the face of the current pandemonium.

Corey and Isabella noticed that a man had exited one of the museum's top floor windows. The man stood on a narrow ledge that couldn't have been more than six inches deep. His back was pressed up against the building, with his palms against the wall. He shimmied his body to the right, and then, with his foot, he reached out to the shoulder of Hera, appearing to gauge the distance. The man adjusted his position on the ledge, swayed back and forth, and then jumped.

Corey and Isabella gasped at the same time.

The man's foot nicked Hera's shoulder, and he lost his balance. As he fell, he grabbed a ruffle of Hera's dress, just under her arm. The rest of his body swung forward, hitting the concrete statue. The man climbed up Hera's dress to her shoulder and held onto the ribbon in her hair. He looked in Zeus' direction and began to walk over Hera's arm, which was the length of a limousine. With his arms extended out like a tightrope walker, the man inched his way across the concrete structure.

Corey and Isabella were mesmerized, and their hearts raced with apprehension. A crowd of people had gathered at the front of the museum and were looking up as well.

The man had made it to the crux of Hera's right elbow when the inconceivable happened. He grabbed his throat with both of his hands. His body waned back and forth for a few seconds, and then it stiffened, while his arms dropped to his sides.

Isabella swiveled her head away and raised her hands to her ears, but she wasn't fast enough.

BOOOMMMM!

The man fell onto the roof of a parked car in front of the museum. The windows on the driver and passenger side exploded like a cannon. Glass scattered across the sidewalk, and for a split second, silence overcame the busy city street. Low murmuring started, then it got louder and louder, and then…the screaming began again.

"Let's go!" Corey said.

Corey and Isabella ran down the alley to the other side of the street and turned left.

"This way," Corey motioned.

They passed the clothing store where earlier, Isabella had observed a woman dressing a mannequin. Isabella stopped, and her hand fell away from Corey's. She saw that the mannequin had toppled over, and the top half of its body was leaning up against the windowpane. Isabella's heartbeat quickened as she walked closer to the glass and saw the woman's shoe in the corner of the display window. A cold feeling of dread came over her, realizing the truth of what she might find. Isabella took a few steps back when she saw the woman lying on the ground behind the mannequin with her cheeks covered in dried blood and foam trickling out of her mouth.

Corey, now standing next to Isabella, gripped her shoulders and turned her toward him. "Listen. We can't stop. We have to find a safe place to hide until this, whatever it is, is over. Do you understand?"

Isabella's face was pale, and her mouth hung open, unresponsive. Her arms sagged lifeless down by her side. She didn't know this woman, but she felt as if she had.

Corey shook her. "Do you understand?"

Isabella didn't say a word. She stared into the window and nodded her head. Corey grabbed her wrist, and they ran.

Corey pulled Isabella into the lobby of his office building, filled with people being directed to the exits by security guards.

"You can't come in here," an older policeman ordered. "We're evacuating the building."

"I have to get my car keys in my office. They have my house key on it. It's right down there, around the corner," Corey protested.

"You have two minutes." The police officer stepped aside.

Corey and Isabella ran through the lobby, passing the elevators, and took a right.

Isabella snapped out of her daze. "Where are we going?"

Corey whispered, "My company has a secure place on the basement floor of this building."

They reached the door to the lower level of the office building, but it was locked. Corey took keys out of his pants pocket, inserted one of them into the keyhole, and unlocked the door. He pushed with his shoulder, but it only opened several inches. He looked at the bottom of the door to see why it was stuck and saw a brown Penny Loafer shoe poking out past the edge. He pulled the door shut and locked it. "We can't go that way."

They ran back the way they had come and stopped just before the lobby. Corey extended his head around the corner and saw the police officer continuing to turn people away from entering the building. Corey looked at Isabella and nodded toward the bright red exit sign at the end of the hallway. They sprinted across the lobby to the exit door, but it was locked. When they turned around to go back, the police officer stood between the connecting hallways.

"Hey! You two! Let's go!" The policeman waved his hand towards the exits.

"I found my keys." Corey shook them in front of the man.

"Yeah, yeah. Just go," the policeman said in disgust.

Corey and Isabella exited the building into streets jammed with cars at a standstill and irate drivers honking their horns and shouting obscenities out their windows.

As they walked down the narrow sidewalk, Corey noticed a man across the street wearing a baseball hat, a black jacket, jeans, sneakers, and carrying something in his hands that looked like the same box from the museum. The man walked into the middle of the street, placed the box down, put one hand in his jacket pocket, paused, and then ran off.

Corey stopped short and put his arm out in front of Isabella, like a parent protecting a child when slamming on the car brakes.

"What?" she asked.

Corey pointed to the box.

Isabella covered her mouth with her hand. "Oh, no!"

They watched as people fled down the street, ignoring the box. It didn't take long before it started happening again. A woman coughed and then grabbed her throat. A man coughed, and a second woman grabbed her throat.

Corey and Isabella stepped back together, then turned and ran in the opposite direction, passing the police officer directing traffic in front of Corey's work building.

"I'll be right back," Corey said.

"No!" Isabella shouted and grabbed his arm.

"I have to let that policeman know about the box. I'll be right back."

"I'll go with you!"

When they reached the police officer, Corey pointed to the middle of the street. "You have to get those people away from that box!"

"Son, what are you talking about?" asked the police officer. "Move on, please."

"Look." Corey grabbed the police officer's shoulders and turned him toward the box.

The police officer glared at Corey. "Do not put your hands on a police officer, young man."

"I'm sorry. But there's something in that box that's killing people!"

The police officer looked in the direction Corey was pointing and saw that people were holding their throats and falling to the ground. "Stay here," he commanded.

As the policeman walked towards the box, he tried to clear a path by pushing his hands out to the sides as if swimming underwater. He occasionally stopped at a body on the ground, checking their pulse to see if they were alive. When he reached the box, the policeman kicked it across the pavement with ease. After it stopped, he moved closer to it, kneeled on one knee, and ripped open the top of the box. He moved his head back and waved his hand across his face as if a foul odor entered his nose. He stood up, put his hands on his hips, and after a few seconds, staggered back, holding his throat with both hands. He stopped, raised his arms out to his sides, like a scarecrow hanging in a cornfield, and tilted his head up, facing the sky.

Corey and Isabella stared, unable to look away, even though they knew what was coming next.

Blood poured from the officer's eyes down the side of his face, and foam rushed from his mouth onto his blue uniform and over his gold badge. His body violently quaked, spraying red and white liquid everywhere. The policeman teetered back on the heels of his shoes, and his toes lifted off the ground. He remained balanced for what seemed like an eternity, then fell backward and hit the ground so hard that his body bounced. When his torso settled in place, his arms moved in unison to the side of his body while the palms of his hands lay flat on the ground.

A crowd of people, who had stopped to watch, shrieked and then scattered like cockroaches. They tripped over each other, and several of them grabbed their throats while running.

As Corey and Isabella stood there, trying to comprehend what just happened to the policeman, the panicking crowd raced toward them so fast that they didn't have time to react. They were swallowed up by thunderous noise and jabbing elbows. Men and women trampled over each other, frantically trying to escape what they couldn't see. People pushed and shoved their way forward, jostling Corey and Isabella around, like clothes in a washing machine, separating them.

Isabella reached for Corey but instead felt warm bodies hustling by, knocking her hand away. She could no longer see him.

She yelled as loud as she could, "Corey!"

Isabella turned in circles, searching for him. Her chest tightened, her breathing became shallow, and tears streaked down her cheeks as dread and panic overcame her.

How was she going to find Corey? Would she ever see him, kiss him again?

CHAPTER 5

The frenzied crowd bulldozed past Isabella, forcing her into the side of a glass building. Her face and chest were pressed against one of the large doors, and she felt the vibration of hundreds of people stampeding in the street. She yanked the vertical handle of one of the doors with both hands, but the immense pressure of bodies ushering by made it challenging to open. She got the door ajar, put her foot between the panes of glass, and wedged her body through the door frame. When she entered the lobby, the glass door slammed shut, echoing in the large vacant space.

Uncomfortable silence rang in her ears as masses of people flashed by the tall panes of glass. A man stumbled in front of the building and fell to the ground. His body got stomped on by other men and women who were holding their throats and foaming at the mouth. Isabella stepped back from the glass doors and turned her head away, not wanting to watch anymore.

In fear of her safety, Isabella scanned the lobby for something to prevent the doors from opening. Next to the check-in counter was an American flag attached to a long metal pole. She raced over, picked it up, and sprinted back across the lobby, dragging the flag on the marble floor. Hands, wedged between the panes of glass, tried to pull the doors open, but the weight of several people leaning up against the doors prevented them from opening. Without thinking, Isabella used the metal part of the flagpole to smash the white-knuckled fingers grasping the edges of the glass. She heard bones breaking and watched droplets of blood splash on the buffed floor. Once the hands released their grip, Isabella inserted the flagpole horizontally through the two brass door handles.

"Let us in!" one woman demanded.

"Are you insane? C'mon open the door, lady," another man begged with desperate eyes.

Isabella backed away, mouthing her apology as if they could read lips. She turned and ran up one of the moving escalators to the second floor. She collapsed into a fetal position on the cold tile and sobbed. Her body shivered as loud gasps of air came one after the other while her chest heaved and her shoulders rose and fell. She closed her eyes, and darkness consumed her. A fatigued sleep took control of her body, and she dreamt of the warm comfort of her mother's arms.

"Isabella? Time for bed, honey!" her mom called up the stairs.

As Isabella's mom climbed the wooden stairs to her daughter's bedroom, she passed family photos hanging above the banister. One particular picture, of Isabella at two years old asleep in her father's arms, put a smile on her face. Her late husband had been a large man who stood over six feet tall with massive arms and a long beard that hung down to his chest. His genuine smile seemed charming and innocent on such a burly man. Isabella had been the joy of his life, and nothing could compare to her.

Reaching the doorway, her mom repeated, "Time for bed, Isabella."

"I know, Mom. Just one more page, please?" Isabella's hazel eyes peeked above the book for approval.

Her mom sat down on her daughter's bed and touched the top of the book. "One more page."

Isabella finished reading, closed the book, and placed it on her nightstand, next to her pink butterfly lamp. She snuggled under her puppy print comforter and pulled it up to her chin, leaving her small head poking out like a turtle.

"Can you sing to me, please?" Isabella asked with her eyes closed.

Her mom tucked the blanket around Isabella and began to sing.

As you lay here throughout the night, darkness surrounds you from the light.

Dreams fill your head while your eyes rest,
taking you on a journey, an imaginative quest.
Go to sleep now while I'm at your side,
protecting you always with loving pride.
You're my angel with a sweet face, I love you
forever and every place!

"Thanks, Mom." Isabella sat up and hugged her mother. "Can you leave the door open a little, please?"

"Sure, honey." Her mother gave Isabella a firm squeeze and tucked her under the covers, then kissed her forehead. "Goodnight. I love you."

"I love you too, Mom." Isabella rolled over on her side and hugged her pillow.

Isabella woke to the nightmare of reality with her arms wrapped around her knees and the side of her face pressed to the marble floor. She quickly sat up when she realized where she was. She wiped the drool from the corner of her lip and could feel the dried tears on her cheeks, causing her skin to feel tight and itchy. Night had descended upon the city, and streetlights gleamed through the tall panes of glass. Isabella stood up, walked over to the railing overlooking the lobby, and saw people in the street wandering past dead bodies covered in foam and dried blood.

She had to find Corey but had no idea where to start. As she descended the escalator stairs, she heard a loud *bang*. Two men were throwing metal trash cans at the front windows of the building. When she reached the last step, she dashed through the lobby toward the elevators. She pressed the buttons on both sides of the walls, desperate for either door to open. When she heard a ding, she ran into the open elevator and, without thinking, pressed the button to the seventh floor. While the doors remained ajar, she heard glass shatter and the loud rumbling of voices.

"Get out of my way!" one man yelled.

"Come on, kids, let's go," a woman ordered.

Isabella pressed her body against the back wall of the elevator, urging the doors to close. The sound of high heel shoes echoed across the lobby. Isabella squeezed into the front corner of the elevator, making every effort not to be seen. She stood on her tiptoes and pressed the palms of her hands against the paneling wall, shielding her body from view. As the elevator doors closed, the angry face of a man came towards her; then, it was gone. Isabella pressed all of the buttons in the elevator so that no one would know where she was headed.

Isabella remained hidden as the doors opened on each floor. The light on the button to the seventh floor disappeared, and the doors opened to a well-lit carpeted foyer. A sign on the wall in front of her read *Levin, Levin, and Marsh, Attorneys at Law,* with an arrow pointing to the left. Isabella leaned forward and put her hands on the elevator doors so they wouldn't close. Poking her head out, she looked in both directions but saw no one. She took two steps into the hallway, turned right, and walked down the hall until she came to another passageway. In one direction were more offices, and at the other end of the hall was an illuminated red *EXIT* sign. She sprinted down the carpeted floor and crashed through the exit door.

In front of her was a long glass corridor connecting the building she was in to the building across the street. She took several steps forward and peered to her left. The ground below her was littered with corpses covered in blood and foam. She saw an open door of a K-9 squad car with a policewoman leaning on the steering wheel, her hand dangling by her side. She hoped that the dog had been able to escape.

Isabella continued walking toward the exit door on the other side of the skywalk. She observed shapes of people moving about in the streets and saw several figures disappear under the glass hallway where she stood. She hurried to one side of the corridor to see if they had come out, but no one had. Isabella dashed back to the other side, pressed her palms against the glass, and looked down to get a better view. When no one had emerged, she continued walking toward the connecting building.

Off in the distance, Isabella noticed a man wandering from one side of the street to the other. He wore black pants and a light-colored shirt with what looked like a piece of cloth wrapped around his mouth and nose. She was perplexed by the man's odd behavior and watched as he stopped in front of a woman leaning up against a streetlamp. The man wrapped his hand with another piece of cloth, lifted her chin, and shook his head back and forth. He placed his hands on his hips and then looked up at the light from the lamppost, exposing his distraught face.

Isabella staggered back several steps — it was Corey!

She pounded on the glass with the palms of her hands, shouting his name, but he didn't respond or even turn around in her direction. Isabella slammed harder with the bottom of her fists, shaking the corridor. Suddenly, the people who had disappeared under the skywalk ran towards Corey.

"Turn around! Turn around!" Isabella screamed.

Two men and a woman, with masks over their mouths, stopped in front of Corey. They appeared to be talking to him while Corey pointed to the dead bodies on the ground, shaking his head. One of the men put his hand on Corey's shoulder and gestured with the other. Corey leaned over, placed his hands on his knees, and bowed his head. The woman in the group touched Corey's back in what seemed like an act of compassion. After several minutes, the men and the woman walked up the street, deeper into the darkness. Corey stood up, wiped his eyes, and followed them.

Isabella panicked. This might be her only chance to get Corey's attention before he disappeared, possibly for good. She knew he couldn't hear or see her, but she had to get his attention somehow.

She ran back through the exit door and saw a fire extinguisher hanging on the wall. She lifted it from its hook and noticed a dark silhouette behind it. Isabella ran to the closest office with a glass door and threw the red metal cylinder through it. *Smash*. Tiny shards of glass shaped like diamonds littered the beige carpet in the office lobby. She maneuvered her hand through the broken glass and unlocked the door. She ran inside the lobby, searching for something with a reflective surface, and on a shelf, behind the reception desk, sat a silver plate that read *Forbes Top 1000*. Isabella grabbed the plate and ran back through the exit door with so much force that it crashed into the wall behind it, leaving a hole in the plaster.

Isabella stopped under a light in the middle of the corridor and looked through the glass to see if Corey was still out there. He was! With both hands, Isabella raised the metal plate to the overhead lamp and tilted it in all directions until a beam of light projected down to the street. When she maneuvered the ray of light around, it uncovered graphic details of a young woman wearing a vibrant pink shirt covered in blood and foam. A fallen child lay next to her, holding a stuffed unicorn in one hand and a man's hand in the other. Isabella's heart sank, and her stomach wretched.

Isabella directed the beam of light towards the woman who had touched Corey's back. It shimmered on the lower part of the woman's dress, like a flashlight at the bottom of a pool. She angled the plate upward, and the light disappeared from the woman's back. Isabella's shoulders burned, and sweat beaded down her forehead into the corners of her eyes, stinging them. She couldn't hold the plate much longer and made one final adjustment with the beam of light, praying Corey would see it.

Isabella shifted the plate's position until a white circle appeared halfway up the woman's back. Corey stopped, put his hand in the beam of light, and wiggled his fingers. He flipped his hand over, and the light disappeared. He looked up at the streetlamp, then back at the woman, and then toward the direction the light came from. He paused, then walked towards the lighted corridor in the sky without looking at the ground.

Elated with relief, Isabella dropped the metal plate to the ground and let her arms sag by her sides. She plunged to her knees, pressed her hands up against the glass, and watched as Corey walked towards the building. She wanted to believe that he was looking at her, so she stood up and waved her arms over her head.

Corey stopped under a streetlamp and stared up in Isabella's direction. He moved into the darkness just below the lighted corridor and put his hands to the side of his eyes. His mouth dropped open, his eyes widened, and then he grinned. He pointed to the building on his left.

Isabella saw the enthusiasm on Corey's face and took off to the other side of the skywalk. She pushed through the exit door so fast that she didn't realize what was in front of her. The palms of her hands broke her fall, and something pressed into her ribs. She looked down and found a sea of bodies covering the floor. Blood had been smeared all over the walls on both sides of the hallway. Isabella crawled over the carcasses on her stomach, and when she reached an open space on the carpet, she stood up. Her hands were covered in blood and foam, so she scrubbed them on her dress until they were almost raw. Staring at the ceiling, Isabella put her hands along the wall to guide her way as she stepped over decomposed bodies and tried not to think of what was at her feet. She reached a corner, looked in one direction, and saw a fluorescent-colored sign decorated with flowers that read *Happy Thoughts Day Care*. Her heart plummeted. She prayed that there had been no children in there today when the horror had begun.

In the other direction, corpses blocked the elevator entrance, leaving Isabella no choice but to take the stairs. She ran to the other end of the hall and burst through the exit door into the stairwell. Holding onto the railing, she hurried down the stairs as if she was floating. Passing the sixth floor, she heard voices but ignored them and continued her descent to the bottom floor. She pushed on the horizontal bar on the lobby door, but it wouldn't budge. She took a few steps back and kicked the door with her the bottom of her foot, but still, nothing happened. She had no choice but to go back through the building and use the stairwell on the other side.

Her thighs burned, and her calves cramped, but she climbed the stairs two at a time. She reached the first floor and pulled on the door, but it was locked. She reached the second floor, but that door was also locked. The only door that opened was on the fifth floor.

Isabella pulled the door ajar, and before entering the hallway, she pressed her ear to the gap of light and listened. She heard voices but couldn't make out what they were saying. She opened the door, walked into the hallway, and tiptoed until she reached an intersection. She ran straight across, sprinted to the end of the hall, took a right, and halted to a stop. Her eyes widened, and she held her breath. Across from her was a man wearing a baseball hat, a black jacket, blue jeans, and black sneakers.

Isabella thought to herself, *Please don't turn around. Corey, where are you?*

74

CHAPTER 6

Corey reached for Isabella's hand, but his attempt was swatted away by bodies rushing by. He tried to maneuver his way in her direction, but unrelenting shoulders and arms of strangers forced him further back.

"Isabella! Isabella!" he shouted.

Corey jumped onto the hood of a car in the middle of the street and looked around the immediate area, but Isabella was nowhere in sight. He saw two glass buildings nearby and hoped that she was in one of them. He leaped off the car and forced his way through the oncoming crowd toward one of the structures. He pulled the heavy glass door open and rushed into the lobby.

"Isabella!" he called out. The sound echoed in the empty space, *Bella...ella...ella.*

She could be anywhere in this abandoned building if she were *even* here. Still, Corey had to check every floor.

Corey sprinted through the lobby to the four elevator doors and pressed the up arrow buttons on both sides of the walls, hoping to speed up the arrival of an elevator. After a long minute, he heard a ding, and the elevator at the far end opened. He ran to it, and inside the metal box were black numbers one through twenty etched into round white buttons. Corey's heart filled with dread when he realized that he would have to get off on every other floor and call Isabella's name, hoping his voice would carry to each level below and above.

Corey pressed the number two on the panel of buttons and then paced back and forth, waiting for the doors to close. After the elevator rose and then stopped on the second floor, he stepped into the hallway and shouted Isabella's name but heard no answer.

Corey sprinted up and down the halls, calling out her name, while his chest heaved with exertion and sweat dripped down his face. He ran back to the elevators, pressed the up arrow button, and the same elevator door opened. Corey ran inside and pressed the button to the fourth floor several times. Brisk air rushed into the small box as the doors closed. He continued this regimen for the first eighteen floors with no results. When the doors to the twentieth floor opened, he stepped into the hallway and shouted Isabella's name again, still with no response.

When Corey reached the end of a hallway, breathless with anxiety and exhaustion, he noticed a man sitting in an office by himself. The man's head was resting on a desk, and his arm dangled by his side. His face didn't appear to have any signs of being sick, but Corey was still apprehensive about approaching him for fear of his own safety, and he wasn't sure how the virus spread. But, what if this man had seen Isabella? Corey had to ask.

When Corey looked closer at the man, a shock of recognition overcame him. Corey had seen his father in this position on many occasions, passed out drunk. He detested his father in that condition because he had been belligerent and aggressive toward his mother. Ordering her around, belittling her, and sometimes becoming violent by throwing things at her.

"Get me another one!" Corey's father crushed the beer can with his hands and threw it at his wife.

Corey's mother jumped up from her chair, hurried into the kitchen, opened the refrigerator door, and took a can of beer off the top shelf.

"When is this going to end?" Corey muttered to his mother while doing his homework at the kitchen table.

"I have no choice, Corey. It's safer for both of us if I just do what he says." She turned to walk back into the living room when she felt a hand around her wrist.

"Mom. Please. This has to stop," Corey pleaded. "Dad's so mean to you when he's like this."

"Honey, listen. Someday this will get better. But right now, I have to do this!"

"No. You don't. We can leave right now. You and me. We'll be ok." Corey's eyes welled up. "I'm leaving for college in the fall, and I'm afraid something terrible will happen to you while I'm gone."

"I'll be fine. I Promise." Corey's mother kissed him on the cheek and walked into the living room.

"It's about time!" his father hollered out. "You're useless!"

Smack

Corey heard his mother whimper. Anger coursed through his veins and the pencil between his fingers snapped on the white sheet of paper. He stood up, slamming his chair into the kitchen sink. He stomped into the living room and stood tall in front of his seated father.

"Enoughhh!" Corey roared.

"Corey. Everything's fine. Please, go finish your homework," his mother begged, as she held the side of her face with her hand.

Corey's father rose from his chair and stood face to face with his son. "You think you're a big shot now. Heading off to college on MY dime!" Spittle flew from his lips onto Corey's face as he spoke.

Corey stood tall, with his body tensed and his fists clenched by his sides. "You don't deserve her. She's too good for you. You're a drunk and a terrible husband!"

With the beer can in one hand, Corey's father swung at his son's face with the other. Corey ducked, then pushed his father back into the chair with so much force, it tipped over. The beer can flew out of his father's hand onto the living room carpet, and his head hit the wooden floor, knocking him unconscious.

"Let's leave, Mom." Corey reached for his mother's hand.

"No." She pulled her hand away. "I can't. He won't survive without me. I have to stay. You go."

"I'm not leaving you!" Corey took both of his mother's hands and looked into her eyes. "Mom. You don't deserve this. You've been abused for too long. You need a life of your own."

His father moaned and struggled to get back up. "Boy! I'm going to kill you!" he grunted. He fell back down with a *thud*.

"I'll be right back." Corey ran into the kitchen, grabbed his homework, backpack, and the keys to his car. "Let's go, Mom."

"I can't, Corey. He needs me." With tears in her eyes, she stared at her dejected husband sprawled out on the floor.

Corey's father lurched to one knee and put his hand on the side of the fallen chair. He glared up at his wife with bloodshot eyes, breathing heavily and slurring his speech. "That's right, woman. You better not leave if you know what's good for you!"

Corey's father stood up and lunged at his son. Corey kicked the ottoman toward his father, who tripped over it and crashed onto the living room table. The four wooden legs exploded like a gunshot, and shards of wood flew across the carpet.

Corey's mom looked at her son and took a deep breath. "Ok."

Corey ran to the front door, with his mother close behind, and yanked it open. Standing with one foot on the porch, and one hand on the doorknob, Corey's mother, looked back at her husband.

"I can't do this anymore, Alan." Then she slammed the door shut.

After many years of rehab, Corey's father got a second chance in life. Perhaps this man, sitting in his office chair, deserved the same fate. Corey knocked on the glass door.

Either the man didn't hear the knock, or he was ignoring Corey. He knocked again, but the man didn't move. Corey turned the cold brass handle on the door, stepped into the lobby, and stopped. He wondered if this man was already dead somehow. He approached the large man and heard sobbing and watched as the man's back rose and fell with each rhythmic breath. His white shirt was darkened under his armpits, and something shimmered in his right hand as it swayed back and forth.

"Hey. You ok?" Corey asked.

The man sat up with a shocked look on his face as if he got caught cheating on a test. "What are you doing here? You need to leave!"

The man stood up, raised his right hand, and pointed a shiny object in Corey's direction. The light from the lobby revealed a gun shaking in the man's grasp. Corey raised his hands over his head.

"I don't know what's going on out there, but you need to leave. Now!" the man shouted.

"Ok. I'm leaving. Sorry." Corey walked backward but stopped when the metal door handle pushed into his lower back.

"No. Wait." The man waved the gun, signaling for Corey to come towards him. "I want to show you something."

With his hands still in the air, Corey took baby steps towards the large man, careful not to make any sudden movements. When he was a few feet from the man, he stopped.

"No. Come closer," the man insisted.

Corey was within arm's length of the gun. The man raised a cell phone in his other hand and showed Corey what was on the screen.

"Uhm, it's paused," Corey said with a trembling voice. His heart was thumping through his chest.

Without taking his eyes off Corey, the man pressed the play button with the pinky finger of his gun hand. Corey wondered if he should make a move to dislodge the weapon but decided against it because there were too many scenarios that would end badly.

The video started playing and showed a woman and a little blonde boy at a park in a sandbox. Corey knew this park. It was right down the street from the building he was currently in.

The woman laughed with the little boy and then spoke into the camera of her cell phone. "Hi, honey."

"Hi, beautiful. What are you doing?" The voice in the video belonged to the man standing in front of Corey.

"Noah and I are at the park. We're building sandcastles. When you're done at work, come join us," she flirted.

The woman adjusted the camera downward to show Noah playing in the sand. The little boy had finished creating two towers and was making a moat to surround a castle.

Corey realized the video must have been pre-recorded because the park was bright and sunny, but night had already fallen on the city.

"This is to keep the bad men out," Noah explained in a high-pitched voice. He couldn't have been more than five or six.

As the man's shaking hand held his cell phone, a bloodcurdling scream emanated from the video. The camera angle shifted from Noah to the sandbox, revealing part of the woman's white sneakers and Noah's blue sneakers. More anguished screams could be heard, then the woman's phone dropped. It landed with the lens facing the blue sky and white clouds.

Corey could hear Noah's voice calling out, "Mom. Mom. You ok?"

Noah repeated the same question several times, but his mother never answered. His arm crossed over the camera view, and his little fingers could be seen tugging at his mother's purple shirt.

Corey heard gurgling coming from the recording, and his heart sank because he knew what was happening. As he lowered his hands, he could still hear the little boy's voice.

"Mom. Mom. What's..." Noah's voice trailed off.

A dark spot, which must have been blood, splattered on the camera lens. As the little boy fell forward over the camera, his arms were at his throat, and his elbows were pressed to his chest, covering what looked like an untucked Thomas the Tank Engine t-shirt. He landed on the cell phone and then vanished out of the picture. The horizontal view from the camera lens displayed the side of the woman's face covered in blood.

The large man paused the video, backed up towards his chair, and sat down. His hands dropped by his sides, and the phone fell onto a plastic mat covering the carpet.

Corey was trembling, and his eyes welled with tears. "I'm so sorry, sir."

The man turned his chair, looked into Corey's eyes, and raised the gun.

Bang!

Corey closed his eyes and grabbed his chest. At first, he wasn't sure if he had been shot or not, but then he realized he didn't feel any pain and was still standing. He heard a dull thud, opened his eyes, and saw the gun on the floor. The man was slumped over in his chair, and the top of his bald head was facing Corey. Blood, covering the side of the man's face and the back of his shirt, pooled on the floor. The man's arms swayed back and forth as they dangled by his sides. Corey heard a woman's voice and realized that the video on the man's cell phone had begun playing again.

Corey backed out of the office, closed the door, collapsed to his knees, and began sobbing. He remained there for a few minutes with his face buried in the palms of his hands. When he stood up, he wiped the tears from his eyes, took several deep breaths, and ran back to the elevators. He kept pressing the down button, waiting for an elevator door to open.

"Hurry up! Let's go," he huffed, half expecting a response.

Ding.

Corey crossed the threshold of the elevator and pressed the lobby button several times. The doors closed in slow motion as if mocking Corey's situation. The elevator reached the ground floor, and before the doors had opened all the way, Corey forced his way through and into the empty lobby. He sprinted across the foyer and exited the front door.

Men, women, and children wandered through the streets, dazed and confused by a terrifying nightmare that had become their reality. This epidemic didn't discriminate toward any one type of individual.

Corey dashed toward the other brightly lit glass building, dodging carcasses covered in dried blood and foam. Approaching the front door, he saw a metal pole lodged between the inside door handles. He walked along the side of the building, scanning the inside of the lobby for Isabella. He looked down with trepidation every few feet to see if any of the dead bodies on the ground resembled her.

He stopped when he saw a woman with golden blonde hair wearing a white sundress, leaning up against the building's last pane of glass. He tried to convince himself that it wasn't Isabella, but he still had to check. He tore the bottom half of his shirt off and wrapped it around his nose and mouth. He ripped off another part of his shirt and swaddled it around his hand. He wasn't sure if the toxin was still contagious after people had died, but he wasn't taking any chances.

His heart moved to his throat as he approached the decaying body. He tucked his unwrapped hand into the pocket of his jeans, and his other hand shook as it moved towards the woman's face. He touched her chin and turned her head towards him. He snatched his hand back when he discovered that it wasn't Isabella. He realized that he had been holding his breath the whole time and released it with a big sigh.

Corey continued down the side of the street, examining any blonde women that he passed. While he was checking one of the dead bodies, he heard footsteps approaching. He turned and saw two men and a woman running toward him.

"Hey, man. You ok?" one man asked.

"I'm trying to find my girlfriend. We were separated a few hours ago." Corey gestured at the bodies littering the ground and choked back tears.

The man touched Corey's shoulder. "That sucks. I'm sorry. We can help you look if you want."

"Do you know what happened?" the woman asked.

"All I know is that some guy came into the museum, placed a box in the middle of the floor, and walked away. Next thing I knew, people were choking and falling to the ground, dead," Corey grumbled.

Corey had seen more carnage than he had ever expected to in his life. He leaned over and put his hands on his knees, trembling, trying to catch his breath.

The woman could hear him crying and put her hand on his back. "It's ok, dear. We'll help you find her."

Corey stood up. "It's not ok. My girlfriend's missing! And today was the day…" He paused for a minute and wiped the tears from his eyes. "I'm sorry. I…I didn't mean to yell."

"I understand. We'll look over here," she replied.

For a few seconds, Corey regarded the bloodbath surrounding him, then shook his head and joined the group of people.

As the four of them walked into the darkness, from the corner of Corey's eye, he saw a light on the back of the woman's dress. It moved in circles and then up and down. He glanced up at the streetlamp and then back at the woman's dress; the light was gone. A few seconds later, it reappeared in the middle of the woman's back.

Corey put his hand up. "Stop. Don't move!"

One of the men stopped and looked back at Corey. "What?"

"There's a light on the back of your dress," Corey said, pointing to the woman.

Corey put the back of his hand in the faint light and wiggled his fingers. When he turned his hand over, the beam of light disappeared. He turned around and walked back the way the strangers had come from. He looked left, then right, but nothing appeared from the windows of the abandoned buildings. He noticed a lighted skywalk that spanned across the street connecting two buildings. He walked closer to the structure, hypnotized by its glow. Corey saw someone waving their arms, and then they stopped, dropped to their knees, and pressed their hands against the glass.

When Corey surveyed the lighted corridor above his head, the brightness from the lamppost made it difficult for him to see. He brought his hands up to the sides of his eyes, shielding as much of the light as possible. He adjusted his vision in the darkness and squinted up at the shape in the corridor. His mouth opened, his heart sped up, and the hair on the back of his neck and arms stood on end. It was Isabella!

Corey pointed to the building on his left and then ran toward the door.

CHAPTER 7

Isabella backed up into the wall behind her, trying not to make a sound. The man's arm hung by his side and in his hand was a small black item. She couldn't see the man's face but saw the cardboard box on the floor between his legs. She froze in fear, knowing what that meant.

The man looked to his right and then moved off in that direction, revealing a glass door with people trapped in the office behind it. Some men and women were pressed up against the door, pounding on the glass and screaming at the man, while their eyes followed him down the hallway. One of the women looked straight ahead and noticed Isabella. Soon, everyone in the room was staring at her.

"Hey! Come help us!" the woman whined.

"Open the door! Get us out of here!" another man demanded.

"Please," another woman begged, as she held a child's hand.

Isabella stood with her hand over her mouth, unable to move, unsure of what to do. She heard a door open, followed by footsteps, and ran back to the hallway she had come from, pressing her back against the wall.

"What are you lookin' at?" a man's voice asked.

Isabella could hear the trapped people screaming and cursing at the man. She poked her head around the corner of the wall and watched as the man picked up the box and stared into the room. He raised the black item in his hand, pressed down with his thumb, and several minutes later, the screaming stopped, and silence filled the hallway. Isabella watched the man disappear back down the corridor from which he had just come from.

Isabella heard the fire exit door slam shut with so much force that it vibrated through the walls. She counted to thirty, then mustered up the courage to turn the corner towards the office.

The first thing she noticed was a door etched with bright gold letters reading *Paul Dorton, DDS*. Behind the sign was a room filled with dead bodies, seeping blood from their eyes and foam from their mouths. Three women sat up against the wall, with their palms flat on the floor, their heads tilted to one side, and their mouths open. An older man sat in a chair, with his arms hanging by his side, slumped over on a desk. Several children could be seen holding their parent's hands.

For a moment, Isabella was overcome with nausea and looked away. She took some deep breaths and didn't want to go any further but approached the office anyway.

Isabella stood inches away from the wooden door and noticed that behind it was a glass door with no handle. She examined the office lobby with greater scrutiny and discovered that the walls and ceiling were lined with glass. She now understood why people couldn't get out. They were trapped inside a glass box!

Isabella took a few steps back from the door and realized that if Corey was in this building, he might be in a room like this, already dead. She had gone through too much to lose him and had no more time to waste. The only way out was through the same stairwell exit the man had just taken. With her fingertips grazing both sides of the walls, she walked down the hallway toward the exit door and paused before opening it. Her hands shook as she pushed the horizontal bar, permitting a sliver of light to shine into her eyes. She opened the door wide enough to step onto the fifth-floor stairwell landing and then eased it shut behind her. Isabella closed her eyes and listened for footsteps, but heard nothing, so she advanced down the cement stairs with extreme caution as if there were landmines placed on each step.

When Isabella reached the fourth-floor platform, she heard a noise from below, and an uneasy feeling washed over her. She pulled the door handle to the fourth-floor hallway, stepped inside, and shut it behind her. She could hear the elevator moving in the shaft, and when it stopped, she proceeded down the carpeted hallway. She turned the first corner, and the man she had seen in front of the glass door on the seventh floor stood in the elevator lobby in front of her. He turned his head and looked straight into her eyes.

Isabella tried to back-pedal but stumbled and fell. As the man moved towards her, she scrambled to her feet, ran back down the hallway, and escaped through the exit door. She scurried to the bottom floor so fast that she didn't remember her feet touching the stairs. She pushed on the metal bar of the exit door, but it was locked! She ran back up one flight of stairs and pulled the first-floor door, but it was locked as well. Climbing two steps at a time, she reached the second floor, and just as she yanked the door open, she saw the man's footsteps coming down the stairs. Isabella sprinted down the hall, past the elevators, and jiggled the doorknobs of every office until one opened.

Isabella ran through the office, passing rows of cubicles taller than she was. The electrical hum of copy machines could be heard in the distance. She bolted to the end of an aisle and searched for a place to hide. Spotting an open office, she snuck inside, closed the door behind her, and locked it. She found herself in a spacious carpeted office with plenty of furniture to hide behind. She moved a leather chair away from the well of the desk, curled up in the center of it, and pulled the chair in close behind her. Her heart was pounding so hard that she was afraid the man would hear it.

A door slammed, and Isabella heard glass break, followed by determined footsteps that grew louder as the man approached the back of the office. Isabella heard the jostling of the doorknob, but it wouldn't open. Sweat dripped down her forehead onto the tip of her nose, and claustrophobia set in. She squeezed her eyes shut and pressed her knees against her chest with her arms clutched around them. She remembered having been this scared when she was a little girl, hiding during a tornado.

"Go! Get in the basement! Now!" Isabella's father had yelled over the swirling wind.

Tumbleweeds rolled across the yard, and wind chimes clanged an unfamiliar cadence. Tree branches snapped and shattered into pieces. The windmill that powered the water system whooshed as it creaked with age.

Isabella scampered down the basement stairs and stood in the middle of the cold, dirt floor, waiting for her parents. Metal shelves surrounding her held enough food and water to last a few weeks. She listened to the howling of the wind as it engulfed the house, causing the yellow storm shutters to clamor off the wooden siding – *thwack, thwack*.

"We'll be fine, honey!" her father shouted. "It's just for a little while, and then it will pass. As long as we're in here, we'll be ok." He pulled Isabella closer to comfort her.

"Your father's right, Isabella. Try to relax. You'll be fine." Her mother looked at her husband with questioning eyes.

Boom!

The bulkhead door tore open, and the wind sprinted down the stairs into Isabella's face. Her hair whirled and danced in the air. Her father struggled to get to his feet and was able to grab the handrail with his left hand. He inched his way toward the stairs that led up to the bulkhead doors. He placed his foot onto the first wooden step and was slammed backward into the cement wall by a gust of wind. He maneuvered his other hand onto the handrail, pulled forward, and put his other foot onto the second wooden step. He reached up, trying to grab the swirling rope attached to the door. He looked back at his wife and shook his head no. She was holding Isabella but knew that she would have to let go of her to help her husband.

"Isabella, I have to help your father!" she hollered.

"No. Don't go!" This was Isabella's first tornado experience. She was scared and wouldn't let go of her mother.

"I have to!" Her mom guided Isabella to a secluded spot behind the chimney, where there was less wind. She motioned for Isabella to stay where she was.

Isabella's mother put both of her hands on one side of the chimney, and with the wind gusting in her face, she forced herself to her feet. She reached for the railing with her hand and, with immense effort, shuffled her feet across the dirt floor. She peered up at her husband, who had managed to grab the rope from one of the metal doors. She could see a look of distress on his face while his arm strained to hold on to the rope. The wind was determined to steal the door and propel it into its funnel, but the strength and courage of Isabella's father would not allow the storm to defeat him.

"Hang on! Let me move up one more step!" Isabella's mom roared.

She gripped the handrail as she reached for the rope with her free hand. The intensity of the wind slammed her body up against her husband. She forced her way up another step and tried to reach for the rope, but her fingers only grazed it.

Her husband shook his head no. "I'll go!"

While grasping the railing, her husband advanced up to the next step and slid his hand higher on the rope. The door rattled in the wind, hanging on by its hinges. He looked down at his wife and nodded for her to move up the stairs. She moved one step closer to him and grabbed the rope with her hand. They yanked downward with all of their strength they could muster. Their faces squinted and their teeth clenched as the bulkhead door inched its way closed. Once the metal door reached halfway, the door slammed shut from the force of the wind's changing direction. Both of them let go of the rope and fell down the stairs onto the dirt-covered ground. Isabella's mom landed on top of her husband, with her face in front of his. They looked at each other and laughed.

Isabella's mom put both of her hands on her husband's chubby cheeks and kissed him. "I love you," she professed.

"I love you too, darling. Now get off me."

Isabella's mom got up and walked over to the chimney, but her daughter was gone. There was no place she could go, so she called out, "Isabella?"

When Isabella didn't respond, her mother got on her knees, crawled behind the chimney, and blindly felt for her daughter. In her search, she found a foot and squeezed the toes.

Isabella opened her eyes and had difficulty adjusting to the dark, confined space. When she was able to focus, she saw that the man who had been chasing her was kneeling in front of the chair with his hand on her toes. Isabella screamed and kicked her feet forward. She heard a *crack,* and the man yelled out in pain. He released Isabella's foot and cupped his nose with both of his hands. Isabella got on her knees, crawled out around the desk, scrambled to her feet, and jetted out of the office.

She raced back the way she had come, bypassing cubicles and offices. When she reached the front office door, she took a right and bolted to the end of the hall, passing the elevators. She thrust open the door to the stairwell, grabbed the handrail, and took the stairs two at a time. She prayed that the door to the lobby on this side of the building would open. It did. Her shoes clip-clopped across the polished floor. She flung open the exit door and ran down the street, screaming Corey's name, hoping that he could hear her if he was still alive.

CHAPTER 8

Corey raced to the door under the catwalk and yanked it open. He bounded into the middle of the empty lobby and searched for the elevators. When he spotted them behind the front desk, he set off across the brown marble floor. He pressed the up button and for that familiar *ding,* but it never arrived. So he raced around the corner to the fire exit door, pulled the metal handle, and scaled the stairs two at a time.

Corey had no idea what floor Isabella was on but knew that it had to be at least the third floor from the height of the skywalk. He opened the stairwell door to the third floor, stepped into the hallway, and stopped dead in his tracks as if he had walked into a closed sliding glass door. The stench of rotten eggs filled his nostrils from decaying cadavers that littered the floor. He couldn't fathom the thought of Isabella being here, but he had to search regardless. He covered his mouth with the crux of his elbow and proceeded down the hall in slow, methodical steps. As he stepped over each blood-covered body, Corey couldn't help but wonder why these people hadn't escaped. He approached a two-way intersection, moved his arm away from his mouth, and called Isabella's name, but heard nothing.

Laying across the threshold of one of the opened elevator doors were the bodies of a man and woman, holding hands. He continued across the elevator lobby and took a left, knowing the other exit door was to the right.

Most of the business offices had their lights on, which aided in Corey's search for Isabella. He opened the first office door, which revealed a small foyer with no reception desk. A sign hanging on one of the walls read *Harden CPA Firm,* and centered on a bookshelf was Newton's cradle surrounded by books on finance and accounting. Each tick of a silver ball hitting another echoed in the deserted lobby, emphasizing the urgency of finding Isabella before it was too late. Corey called out, yet again, heard nothing. He exited the CPA office and continued down the hall.

"Come on, Isabella. Where *are* you?" he pleaded.

Corey stepped into the foyer of the next business and noticed portraits of American presidents lining the walls. He called Isabella's name, but silence filled his ears. Just as he was about to leave, he heard a scream from outside of the building. He ran into the vacant office in front of him, pressed his hands against the window, and peered through the darkness. He saw a woman, with long blonde hair and a flowered dress, running and glancing over her shoulder as if she were being chased. It was Isabella! Then, from out of the shadows came a man, sprinting after her.

Corey bolted out of the office to the end of the hallway and then through the fire exit door. He jumped to the landing of each floor, bypassing the five stairs of each flight. He reached the ground floor, slammed through the stairwell door, and raced across the lobby, with his arms outstretched ahead of him, in anticipation of pushing through the exit door. The brisk night air engulfed his body as he strained himself to reach Isabella.

"Isabella!" Corey yelled.

Even in the ensuing chaos and noise all around her, Isabella recognized the voice. She stopped and turned in the direction of this familiar sound and saw Corey racing towards her.

The man chasing Isabella stopped and turned towards Corey, but he didn't have time to react. Corey buried his right shoulder into the man's midsection, wrapped his arms around the man's waist, picked him up, and slammed him to the ground. The man landed on his back with a *thud*. His arms flew up over his shoulders, and his head struck the pavement. Corey stood up and stared at the man, who appeared stunned and unable to move.

Corey looked up at Isabella and ran to her. She jumped into his arms and wrapped her legs around his waist, clinging to him like a barnacle. He embraced her, feeling the pounding of her heart against his chest. After several seconds, Isabella opened her eyes and noticed that the man Corey had knocked to the ground was walking in their direction.

"He's coming!" Isabella released her grip on Corey and dropped to her feet.

Corey turned to face the man while putting his hand on Isabella's waist and edging her body behind his. Isabella put both of her hands on Corey's back and peeked over his shoulder.

"Be careful," she whispered.

"What do you want?!" Corey chided.

The man didn't respond, just increased his pace walking towards them. His furrowed eyebrows and his blood-stained nose conveyed his intent. When he was about ten feet away, he stopped, reached into his pocket, and pulled out the black item Isabella had seen earlier. He raised it in the air and pressed a button with his thumb, but nothing happened. The man stared at Corey and Isabella for a moment and then ran off.

When the man was out of sight, Corey turned back to Isabella, "I can't believe I found you. I thought I'd *never* see you again." His throat tightened with emotion, and tears welled up in his eyes.

"I'm so sorry we got separated," Isabella said with a trembling voice.

"You don't have to apologize. I tried so hard to find you. I wasn't giving up." He put both of his hands on the sides of her face and kissed her.

Isabella welcomed his soft lips and tender embrace. She put her arms around his neck, placed her head into his left shoulder, and sobbed with exhaustion and gratitude.

Not wanting to let her go, Corey softly spoke. "Isabella, we have to go. We need to get to my car and find out if your mom is ok."

Nodding, Isabella let go of Corey and looked up at him, smiling through tear-filled eyes, "I'm still amazed that you found me. How did you know where I'd be?"

Corey wiped the tears from her cheeks with his thumbs. "Well, I knew you wouldn't go far because you don't know the city. So, I took a chance with the closest buildings. We have so much more to talk about, but we have to go."

Corey took her hand, and they headed back in the direction of his office. It wasn't a far walk, and when they reached his building, they saw remnants of smoke dancing in the air from the hood of a small white car that was entangled with a grey SUV in front of the parking garage.

"Maybe we can move the car out of the way," Isabella proposed.

"Check if the keys are in it."

Isabella got into the driver's seat and reached for the keys in the ignition, but they were gone. "Nothing here."

Corey looked at Isabella. "I want you to stay in the driver's seat, put the car in neutral, and I'll try to push it out of the way."

"Ok." Isabella put her hand on the steering wheel, her foot on the brake, and shifted the car into neutral.

Corey stood in front of the car, placed his hands on the hood, and braced himself. "Ok. Release the brake," he instructed.

After removing her foot from the brake pedal, Isabella could see that Corey struggled to move the car and shifted the gear selector into park. "What's wrong?"

Corey looked down at the front of the white car. "The car's bumper is stuck under the bumper of the SUV, so we have to move the SUV first. Which means we also have to remove the driver."

"What?" Isabella questioned. "No way. He's all covered in blood and foam. He could still be contagious. No!"

Corey approached the SUV and looked at the large man slumped over in the driver's seat. He glanced back at Isabella. "It's the only way I can get my car out of the garage. I'm sorry. We have to."

Isabella shook her head no. "Why don't we just push him out from the passenger side?"

"We can't. The door won't open. It got pretty banged up from the accident."

"Fine! You need to cover your mouth and nose. You can't get sick. You can't do that to me!" Isabella demanded.

Corey covered his mouth and nose with a piece of his shirt and then walked around to the driver's side of the SUV. When he opened the door, a pungent odor rose from the driver's seat, making Corey's eyes water; the man had urinated himself.

The obese man's stomach rested on the steering wheel, while his massive arm, the width of his upper body, hung down by his side. His pant leg creases showcased layers of fat, while his face and shirt were covered in blood and foam. Corey had no choice but to reach around the man's large stomach to undo the seatbelt.

Corey stepped onto the lift ledge, grabbed the back of the driver's seat with one hand, and reached across the man's bulging belly with the other. The seat belt was just out of reach, so Corey had to place part of his upper body on the man's stomach. Putrid air wafted from the man's mouth, and red spittle flew from his lips onto Corey's shirt. Corey felt the tip of the belt buckle and pushed with his fingers, trying to dislodge the inserted metal piece but was unsuccessful. He leaned in further, causing more spittle to fly from the man's mouth, landing on Corey's cheek. He was so close and couldn't wipe it away just yet.

Click. The seat belt unfastened.

Corey jumped out of the SUV, tore off his shirt, and used the inside of it to wipe the droplets of blood from his face. He shuddered, and the hair on the back of his neck stood up.

"Are you ok?" Isabella asked.

Wiping the blood off his face, Corey remarked, "Yeah. I got some of his blood on my clothes. That's all." He didn't tell her the truth because he knew she would panic.

Corey wrapped his blood-stained shirt around the man's arm and pulled. The massive body didn't move, so Corey pulled harder but was still unable to budge him. Isabella walked around to the driver's side of the SUV.

"No!" Corey shouted. Waving her off with his right hand. "You don't want to see this."

If Corey had only known what Isabella had gone through these past few hours, he would have welcomed her help.

Corey continued to struggle, trying to pull the man from the driver's seat of the SUV. With each yank of the man's arm, drips of urine oozed from the seat cushion. After several Herculean attempts, the man fell to the ground, and his body remained in the seated position.

The vehicle's seat was sopping wet with blood and urine, but someone had to sit on it to shift the SUV into neutral. Corey stood on the lift ledge and spotted a blanket and some coats in the back seat. He climbed over the driver's seat, careful not to let any of his clothes touch the dampened cushion, and grabbed the jackets and the blankets. He layered them on the driver's seat, then stepped out of the vehicle.

"Ok, I've covered the seat. Go ahead. Hop up and get ready to shift the SUV into neutral." Corey said.

"What? You want me to sit on that seat covered in blood and urine. NO! You do it, and I'll push." Isabella walked around to the front of the SUV, placed her hands on the hood, and nodded. "Let's go."

Conditioning himself against the revolting but necessary task, Corey climbed into the SUV and sat on the driver's seat. He could feel the wetness through the extra layers of material, or perhaps it was all in his mind. He shifted the SUV into neutral and nodded at Isabella to push.

Isabella leaned her body against the front of the SUV and pushed as hard as she could, but it wouldn't budge. She paused to rest, then tried again; still, it wouldn't move. In dismay, she walked around to the driver's side door of the SUV.

"You push," she griped.

Corey got out of the vehicle without saying a word and walked around the back of the SUV. He stopped when he got to the rear bumper, looked at her, and spoke. "You want…."

Isabella held her hand up, facing Corey. He smiled, then continued on his way.

Isabella grabbed the steering wheel and stepped on the ledge. She wasn't in the seat yet, but her nostrils twitched from the overpowering stench. She squirmed as she sat down, and without looking up at Corey, she shifted the vehicle into neutral.

With his hands on the hood of the SUV, Corey braced one foot in back of him and the other foot just under the front bumper and pushed. His muscles bulged and strained with effort. The metal from the two bumpers scraped like a filing cabinet being dragged across the cement. Exhausted, he halted his efforts and shook out his arms as the SUV rolled back to its original position. He pushed it forward, let it roll back, and pushed it forward again. Back and forth, it rocked as the metal tore apart from each vehicle. Corey gave it one final push, dislodging the bumper of the SUV from the white car. Isabella let the vehicle roll back a little, then put it in park. She hopped out of the driver's seat so fast, Corey thought she had fallen.

"Are you ok?" he asked.

The back of her white dress was stained in blood, and the lower portion of her long blonde hair was splattered with specks of red. Isabella stormed over to the white car, sat in the driver's seat, shifted the car into neutral, and waited for Corey to push.

Corey walked over to the front of the car and moved the vehicle back with ease.

Isabella put the car in park and walked back to Corey. "Can we go now?"

They ran into the parking garage, and Corey remotely unlocked the doors, but this time he didn't go to Isabella's side because she was already in the passenger seat. Sitting in front of the steering wheel, Corey paused for a moment, then reached in the back to get his coat. "Do you want this?"

"No. I'm fine." Isabella blinked back tears and looked out of the passenger window.

Corey touched her shoulder. "We've both been through a lot tonight, and I'm glad we're here together. We're going to make it through this." He kissed the top of her head.

"I should call my mom. She must be worried."

"She may not even know what's going on in the city. She's probably doing chores around the farm," Corey assured her.

"I hope you're right." Isabella took her cell phone from the center armrest console and dialed her mother's cell phone. She let it ring until it went to voice mail and then hung up.

Corey pressed the push-button ignition, shifted the car into drive, and started to pull out of the garage when he slammed on the brakes unexpectedly. Isabella flopped forward, dropping her cell phone, and braced her hands against the passenger side dashboard. She half-looked at Corey, wondering why he had stopped short. Corey's body was frozen, and the blood had drained from his face. Isabella turned her head in the direction of Corey's gaze and saw the man, who had chased Isabella, standing in front of the exit of the garage.

CHAPTER 9

Isabella's mom was about to sit down in front of the television to eat dinner when it dawned on her that she had forgotten to fill the horse's water trough in the barn.

"Dang it, Helen. You keep forgetting things," she said aloud. Her memory wasn't like it used to be. She placed her dinner plate and glass of water on the coffee table in the living room. She grabbed her jacket off the coat rack and stepped out onto the wooden porch, letting the screen door smack against the wooden frame.

The night air was brisk, and the sky, filled with stars, provided a clear path to the barn. Wolves and coyotes howled to one another under the full moon, and bats flew overhead. Each step Helen took left an imprint of her boots in the muddy path. As she pulled open the large red barn door, a warm gust of air blew past her.

The first stall housed a young quarter horse named Maxi. Helen pulled the stable door open, patted his neck, and picked up a metal bucket in the corner.

"Be right back," she said.

She left the barn door open, walked over to the watermill, submerged the metal bucket, and filled it to the top. As she carried it back in her right hand, water sloshed over the brim onto her boots. She entered the barn and placed the full bucket of water on the dirt floor in front of Maxi's stall. She shook her arm and rubbed it, trying to get the circulation flowing again.

"Old age is not for me." Helen sighed.

After a minute or so, she picked up the bucket and was about to pour water into Maxi's trough when she heard a low growl behind her. Her heart raced, and her body tensed. She cursed herself for not closing the barn door. She turned her head and peeked over her shoulder to see what ravenous creature was in there with her.

In the doorway of the barn stood an enormous gray wolf, the biggest one she had seen in years. Its massive head hung low, while its deep dark eyes glared at her. Canine teeth protruded from its upper lip as white foam dripped from the side of its mouth onto the dirt. The animal's fur stood up on its back, forming a shark-like fin down its spine. Its tail swung side to side as it moved towards her, one massive paw at a time.

Horses scurried around in their stalls, creating a thunderous clamor, while pigeons flew from the hayloft through the small opening at the top of the barn.

Helen wouldn't be fast enough to get into Maxi's stall, so she would have to use the metal bucket filled with water to defend herself. She gripped the handle with both hands and eyed the beast as it inched closer.

The wolf's growl revved like a car engine, and it lowered its head. The wolf stopped, crouched, and with its yellow teeth bared, leaped toward Helen. Without thinking, Helen turned, swung her arms forward, and threw the bucket of water at the wolf while it was in midair. The metal pinged off of its nose, and water splashed all over its body and into its mouth. The animal landed on all four paws, shook its head, and began to growl again. Its fur, saturated with water, revealed defined muscles on the front and back of its legs. With its dagger-like teeth exposed and its tongue hanging to one side, the wolf continued stalking its prey.

Helen backed away, holding the palms of her hands up toward the enormous creature. She continued down the length of the barn until she noticed an open door to one of the stalls. Keeping both of her eyes fixated on the wolf, Helen backed into the stall, passing a pitchfork impaled into a bale of hay. She couldn't be sure if she would reach it in time before the wolf attacked, but she had no choice. Just as she lunged for the pitchfork, the wolf sprang at her again.

Helen raised the pitchfork just in time to fill the wolf's mouth with the wooden shaft. The beast bored down on her, gnawing on the wood, peppering splinters onto her face like a wood chipper. She held the wolf at bay, but her arms were burning from the pressure of its weight. She thrashed her legs, kicking dirt and hay on the ground, and then heard a whimper when her knee connected with the wolf's ribs. She turned her head to avoid the wolf's chomping teeth inches from her face. Her arms were losing their strength, and the wooden shaft was about to break.

Suddenly, Helen felt the animal's weight lessen on her arms, and the wolf halted its incessant attack. It staggered back, shaking its head. White foam flew from its jaw, and blood seeped from the corners of its eyes. With its tail between the back of its legs, the creature placed the tip of its nose on the ground and dragged it along the hay-filled floor.

Helen crab-walked back with the pitchfork's tines in one hand and the broken shaft in the other. Staring at the wolf, she stood up and edged sideways toward the opened stall door. She watched as the wolf stumbled and thrashed into the sidewalls. She didn't know what was happening to the wolf but felt pity for him.

The wolf fell over with a *thump*. Blood continued to flow from its eyes while foam oozed out of its mouth onto the dirt-covered ground. Staring up at Helen, it whined as if to say, *help me*.

Then, it all stopped. An eerie silence overcame the barn. The wolf lay motionless with blood covering its eyes and foam coating its mouth and snout. Its paws were neatly crossed over one another, and its pointed ears sagged down on top of its giant head.

Helen's eyes brimmed with tears wondering why she had any compassion for this animal who would have killed her. She made her way to the adjoining stall and grabbed a riding blanket. She walked over to the wolf, lying in a pool of blood, and draped the blanket over its lifeless body. She turned her back to the dead animal, exited the stall, and closed the door.

Helen looked at the water bucket, still rolling back and forth on the ground, and wondered how that could have killed the wolf when it only hit him in the nose. She noticed that the wet, darkened area around the bucket had a shiny film to it. She rushed out of the barn and ran toward the watermill. When she got there, she found a fox lying on the ground next to the trench, its eyes bloodied and its tongue resting on the grass. She examined the water and then smelled it, but nothing seemed out of the ordinary. There was no cloudy film or swirls of abnormality on top. She picked up a twig, stirred it in the water, and when she removed it, she found no discoloration on the wet part of the stem. Helen turned off the pump to the mill as a safety precaution, stopping all water flow in the trench.

Helen sprinted back to the house and straight to the kitchen sink. She lifted the faucet handle and examined the stream of water flowing down the drain. She took a glass from the cupboard, filled it, and then held it up to the overhead light. She saw tiny particles floating throughout the still water. She dropped the glass in the sink, shattering it.

"Isabella?"

Helen checked her pockets for her phone, but they were empty. She knew she had it with her when she had gone to the barn. She retraced her steps across the mud, combing the ground from side to side as she went. Inside the barn, she scanned the hay and dirt-covered floor but didn't see her phone. She checked Maxi's stall but didn't find anything. She paused, then looked in the direction of the wolf's dead body. Even though she knew the wolf was dead, her heart still raced with apprehension.

Helen approached the stall door and looked through the vertical metal bars at the lifeless creature under the blanket. She lifted the handle, unlocking the stall door, and let it swing open past her. With her eyes affixed on the carcass, she walked into the stall, got on the floor, and sifted through straw and dirt. At last, she found her phone and saw that there had been one missed call from Isabella. While on her knees, she looked over at the shape under the blanket and crawled over to it. With her hand trembling, she put her palm on top of the dead animal's chest and felt the warmth of its body, but not the rise and fall of its breath. She got to her feet, turned her back on the beast, and walked out of the stall, shutting and locking the door behind her.

She hurried back to the house and turned on the television to see if anything about the city's water supply was being broadcasted. A young female reporter with jet black hair and a piece of cloth covering her mouth and nose appeared on the screen. With a microphone in her hand, she looked at the camera and spoke.

"We are at the city's water treatment plant where the police have apprehended several men who were contaminating the water supply. The police are urging all residents to *not* use any water under any circumstances, including well water."

Helen dialed her daughter's cell phone and listened to its ring. When it went to voicemail, she hung up. She called Isabella again and got the same result, but left a voice mail this time. "Hi honey, it's mom. Are you ok? I'm watching the news, and something's going on with the city's water supply. So please don't drink or touch it. Call me as soon as you can."

As Helen continued watching the news, the camera panned to an elderly couple holding hands and sitting on the sidewalk in front of a building. Helen's eyes widened. "Mrs. Parker!"

Helen dashed out of the house, across the yard, and ran up the wooden stairs onto the porch of her neighbor's house. She knocked on the door, but there was no answer. She knocked again, harder this time, but still no response. She hurried to the back of the house and knocked on the glass of the wooden door; no one answered. She put her hand on the doorknob, turned it, and pushed the door open.

Standing in the doorway of the kitchen, Hellen called out, "Hello? Mrs. Parker? Are you here?" Stillness echoed through the house.

Helen stepped inside the kitchen and closed the door behind her. The kitchen table was littered with newspapers and coupon clippings, and a chair was pushed back from it. On the counter sat an open loaf of bread, a knife, and an uncapped jar of mayonnaise. She walked through the kitchen, into the hallway, and when she reached the living room entrance, she was hesitant to look around the corner. When she poked her head past the wooden edge of the archway, there was Mrs. Parker, lying on her back in the middle of the carpeted floor. The older woman's eyes and cheeks were covered in dried blood, and foam had dripped out of her mouth onto her blue-flowered nightgown. Her hands were by her side, with her thumbs pointing into her thighs. Next to Mrs. Parker's feet was a broken plate, a half-eaten sandwich, shards of glass, and a dark stain on the carpet, confirming Helen's worst fear.

Helen had known Mrs. Parker for forty years and couldn't just leave her lying on the floor. She went into the kitchen, grabbed a dish towel, and wrapped it around her nose and mouth. She put on rubber gloves from under the kitchen sink, gathered up a broom and dustpan, and went back into the living room. She swept up the glass and food from the carpeted floor and emptied it into the kitchen trash barrel. She took a bowl from a cabinet and filled it with soap and warm water. She took another dishtowel from the closet and walked back into the living room.

Helen's eyes welled up as she knelt next to her dear friend. She closed Mrs. Parker's eyelids and gaping mouth. She washed the woman's face, making sure not to press too hard. Each wipe uncovered deep lines, accentuating her gentle face. Her lips were curled up in the corners, forming a half-smile.

After Mrs. Parker's face was clean, Helen emptied the bucket of bloody water into the bathroom toilet. Upon leaving, she noticed a bathrobe hanging on the back of the door and took it with her.

Helen rolled Mrs. Parker on to her side and slid the woman's arm into one of the sleeves. She repeated the same process with the other arm. She placed Mrs. Parker on her back and tied the belt around her waist. Then with all her strength, Helen hoisted the lifeless body onto the couch and crossed the woman's arms over her sunken chest. She put a pillow under Mrs. Parker's head and covered her body with the floral blanket from the back of the couch. She leaned in, kissed her long-time neighbor on the forehead, turned off the lights, and left through the back door.

Helen removed the towel from her face and looked up at the full moon, wondering how this could have happened and why.

Helen looked at her phone, but there were still no calls from Isabella, so she hurried back to her house. On the television screen, a male reporter shouted into his microphone. "Whatever you do, don't come into the city! Stay away at all costs!"

The television camera panned the city streets, focusing on abandoned cars smashed into telephone poles and buildings. The lens zoomed in on a black car with four people inside; a man in the driver's seat, a woman in the passenger seat, and two kids in car seats. Their faces were covered in blood, with their mouths open and their eyes staring straight ahead.

Helen couldn't watch anymore and switched the channel to another live broadcast. This coverage showed people running through the streets, wearing bandanas on their faces, and looting local stores. A female reporter pointed to a specific area on the street and spoke with a sense of urgency.

"There. Down there. What's that?" she asked.

The camera shifted its angle and zoomed in on a man wearing a baseball cap, standing in front of a parking garage entrance.

CHAPTER 10

Corey kept his eyes focused on the man blocking the garage exit. He whispered to Isabella, "Buckle in."

Isabella slid her belt buckle over her body without shifting her gaze and clicked it into the locking mechanism.

Corey attempted to intimidate the man by revving the car's engine, but he didn't budge. Corey revved the engine again, this time rocking the car forward, but still, the man held his ground.

"Hang on," Corey muttered.

Isabella clenched the overhead passenger grab handle with one hand and the center console with the other. She pushed her head against the headrest and her back against the leather seat.

Corey released the brake and pinned the gas pedal to the floor. Isabella squeezed her eyes shut and felt the vehicle heave forward. She heard two heartbeat thumps as the car's wheels rolled over the man's body and then smashed through the horizontal bar across the garage exit, snapping it in half. The vehicle veered out of control and careened off the cement sidewalk into the white car that had been dislodged from the SUV. The driver's side airbag exploded in Corey's face hard enough that he lost consciousness.

Isabella's airbag didn't go off, but her body jolted forward with such force that her seat belt strap slapped her windpipe. She grabbed her throat and gasped for air. When she looked at Corey, he was slumped over on the steering wheel with blood dripping down the side of his face.

Isabella touched his shoulder. "Corey? Corey?" she called in a raspy voice.

He was unresponsive. She unbuckled her seat belt, opened her door, and ran around to the driver's side of the car. After opening Corey's door, she eased him back against his seat and noticed a deep gash above his eyebrow. She ripped off a clean part of her dress and pressed it against the cut, stopping the flow of blood. She glanced back in the direction of the garage and saw the man lying on the ground, motionless.

Turning back to Corey, she asked, "Are you ok? Can you hear me?"

"Ow." Corey raised his hand to his forehead, but Isabella grabbed his wrist before he touched the open wound. She didn't want to get it infected, which seemed ironic given the current situation.

"Your forehead is cut pretty bad. There's a deep gash just above your eye. Do you have a First Aid kit?" Isabella asked.

Corey winced. "In the trunk." Corey pressed the trunk button next to the steering wheel.

Isabella walked to the back of the car and found a jumbled mess of unopened bottles of water, an umbrella, and golf clubs. She rummaged through the items searching for a red and white box, and when she found it, she grabbed a bottle of water as well.

Corey, still dizzy from the collision, attempted to step out of the car, but when he stood halfway up, his body swayed, and Isabella caught him under his arms just as he was about to topple over. She sat him back down in his seat. "Not so fast."

"Where is he?" Corey asked, turning his head.

"Hey, don't move. Let me take care of your cut first." Isabella looked to her right and nodded without saying a word.

She handed Corey the water, opened the medical kit, removed a large bandage, and peeled back the paper wrapping. She removed the cloth from the gash above his eye, and blood trickled down the side of his nose. She placed the bandage over the cut and smoothed it to his forehead.

When she had finished, Corey poked his head out of the driver's side door and saw the man lying face down on the ground in a pool of blood. The man's baseball cap lay upside down a few feet away from his body.

Corey looked back at Isabella. "I'm sorry. I didn't think I had a choice."

Taking Corey's hand, she looked him in the eyes. "*We* didn't have a choice, and you're going to need stitches when this is over. Now drink some water."

After Corey drank half of the water, Isabella helped him out of the car, and they walked towards the lifeless body.

Corey pushed the man's shoulder with his foot, making sure he was dead. "What do you think that thing he was holding was?"

"I don't know, but I saw him holding it earlier, in the hallway of a building. He was standing in front of a glass door."

Corey knelt beside the body, reached into the man's jacket pocket, and pulled out the black device. It was oval-shaped with smooth, curved edges that contoured to a person's hand. There was also a red button on top, which may have been an activation switch.

"What do you think it does?" Isabella questioned.

"Not sure, but whatever it does, I don't want to be associated with it." Corey wiped the device with his shirt, making sure to remove his fingerprints, and then threw it into the bushes next to the garage.

"I want to call my mom again."

Isabella turned and ran back to the passenger side of Corey's car. She searched for her phone and found it lodged between her seat and the armrest console. A red battery symbol blinked in the phone's top right corner, indicating that she had three-percent battery life left. She dialed, and her mom answered.

"Mom! You're home! Thank God. I was so worried about you. Are you ok?" Isabella looked at Corey, smiling. "Yes, Mom. I'm fine. I'm here with him now. We're trying to find a way out of the city. Mom? Mom?" Isabella looked down at her phone.

"Is she ok?' Corey asked.

"I think so. My stupid phone died."

"Well, at least she knows you're alive. I'm sure she's happy about that. Plus, you told her that we're trying to get home." Corey put his arms around Isabella. "You're freezing! Let's go to my office and get you a coat. I'll see if I can find the keys to the company car."

"But what if we run into another one of those guys? We can't take that chance."

Corey took Isabella's hand. "If there's any danger, we'll leave. No question."

"Ok," Isabella agreed.

They walked back through the parking garage, bypassing the dead man on the ground. When they got to the elevator, Corey pressed the up arrow button, and a door dinged. Once they were inside the metal box, Corey pressed his work badge to the bar code reader, and the eleventh-floor button lit up.

As the elevator climbed up the noisy shaft, Isabella took Corey's hand and nestled the side of her face into his shoulder. When the doors opened, a rotten stench invaded the small compartment. Two decomposing bodies lay on the ground opposite the elevator doors.

Standing still, Corey held one finger to his lips, then touched his ear, signaling Isabella to listen. He stepped across the threshold and looked in both directions but saw no one. They stepped out of the elevator, headed left, but stopped after a few feet. They leaned up against the wall, and Corey peeked around the corner to see if the coast was clear.

"I can see people moving in an office on the left. We should see if we can help them," he whispered.

Isabella shook her head in disagreement. "We should leave."

"What if it was you in there? Wouldn't you want someone to help you?" Corey asked.

Isabella knew he was right, but she just wanted to go home.

They slinked along the wall, and when they got in viewing distance of the office, several men and women noticed them and started pounding on the glass. Corey gestured for them to be quiet by pressing his finger to his lips.

"Help us!" one woman shouted.

"You have to open the door," a man chimed in.

One of the women pointed to the middle of the door. "There's no handle. You have to get us out of here!"

Isabella took a few steps back and shook her head back and forth.

"What's wrong?" Corey asked.

"No. No. No." She grabbed Corey's wrist.

"What's wrong?"

"I've seen this before in one of the buildings I was in. The man that chased me stood in front of a glass door like this. It had no door handle on the inside, either. He had that black thing in his hand…there were bodies on the floor…blood everywhere." Isabella began to hyperventilate and reached for Corey's hand, trying to pull him away. "We have to go!"

Corey pulled his hand out of her grip and walked towards the door. "Let's see if we can get them out first."

Corey turned the handle of the wooden door, and it opened. He moved closer to the glass door and kicked it with the bottom of his foot, but it just vibrated against the wall. Corey examined the frame of the wooden door. "Look at the top. There's no connection from the glass door to the building frame. It's separated from the rest of the structure. Nothing is securing it." He looked back at Isabella. "It's the same on all sides. Like...some sort of glass box."

Isabella covered her mouth with one hand and pointed at the office with the other. Corey turned his head back to the door and saw that some of the people had grabbed their throats and were reeling back and forth. Others picked up chairs and threw them against the glass door, but they ricocheted back. Men and women clawed past each other, desperate to escape the room. A woman, foaming at the mouth, slammed into the door, smearing white liquid across the glass. A man crashed to the floor as blood seeped from his eyes. Another man tripped and fell, hitting his head on the corner of the desk, squirting blood from the side of his head onto the glass door.

Corey and Isabella watched in horror, unable to take their eyes off the screaming victims. One by one, bodies fell over onto their backs, with their hands by their sides. Then...silence. All of the men and women, now on the floor drenched in blood and foam, stared up at the glass ceiling with lifeless eyes.

Corey grabbed Isabella's hand. "We need to leave. Now!"

"Where are we going? Why aren't we taking the elevator?"

"Because if anyone is here, they'll hear it! We'll take the stairs. They're just past my office. We'll stop for the keys."

They started down the hall, and then Corey stopped.

"What is it?" Isabella asked.

"There's a jacket in there you can wear." Corey pointed to a coat rack in the corner of an office lobby. He turned the doorknob, and it opened. "I'll be right back."

"No! I am not losing you again! I'm fine. I don't need a coat."

"Come with me then."

They snuck into the office and stood on a large area rug centered in the middle of the lobby. Corey walked over to the coat rack next to a reception desk, unhooked a long black jacket, and handed it to Isabella.

Thank you, Isabella mouthed. The coat hung well below her knees, and the length of the arms extended past her fingertips.

They were about to leave when Isabella noticed a suit hanging in a nearby office. She tugged at Corey's arm and nodded her head in that direction. Stepping off the rug, they walked toward the office. Corey let go of Isabella's hand and tilted his head sideways, signaling he was going in.

Corey crossed into the office, reached behind the door, took the jacket off the hook, and to his surprise, there was a white shirt hanging under it. He took off his blood-stained jacket, dropped it on the floor, and dressed in the fresh, clean clothes.

They hurried down the hallway to Corey's office, where he scanned his badge against the electronic security reader, and they walked into the lobby. Corey stepped behind the reception desk, opened a drawer, and sifted through its contents. After a minute, he slammed the drawer shut. "Damn it. They're not here."

They exited his office and followed the length of the corridor, through the exit doors. Isabella thought to herself, *back in the stairwell, again.*

Corey sprinted down the cement stairs, with Isabella close behind. When he reached the bottom floor, he ran into the exit door with so much force that it recoiled back into his hand. He winced in pain and grabbed his wrist.

"Are you ok?" Isabella asked.

"Yeah." Corey knew his wrist was broken or sprained, but he couldn't tell Isabella because she would worry, and he needed her to be strong until they reached somewhere safe.

Corey and Isabella sped through the lobby and exited the building into the cool night air.

Corey looked at the carnage covering the streets and shook his head in disgust. "How did this happen?"

"I don't know, but you said we'd be ok." Isabella touched the side of Corey's face. "Let's find a car."

They wandered the lonely streets, peering inside unoccupied vehicles, taking every precaution to avoid the trauma of removing a dead body from a car again.

"That red minivan." Isabella ran to the vehicle, checked all of the windows for bodies, and found it empty.

"I'll check to see if there are keys in it." Corey opened the driver's side door and looked at the ignition. "They're gone."

"I'll check another..."

Corey interrupted Isabella, "Do you hear that?"

"Hear what?"

"Voices."

Isabella turned her head in different directions and listened. "I hear them now."

"Quick. Behind the van," Corey instructed.

CHAPTER 11

"What time are we meeting tonight?" a tall, lanky man with a protruding chin asked.

"Midnight. At the water station," a large muscular man barked. "Is everything all set?"

"Yeah, I'm good," the first man responded.

A third man, with a baby face and a slim build, piped in. "Just about."

"What do you mean, *just about*? Everything has to be…" The large man's voice trailed off. "What in the hell?" he murmured.

The other men looked up and turned their heads to see what had distracted the large man. A bloodied body lay face down in front of a parking garage. The three men ran over to it.

The muscular man kneeled beside the motionless figure and rolled the body onto its back. Shocked recognition came over his face, and his heart jumped into his throat. The body belonged to his younger brother, Ed.

The dead man's eyes remained open, staring up at the sky. His face, covered in blood, was caved in on the left side, revealing broken bones in his nose and jaw. His left elbow protruded from his black jacket, and his left leg was twisted unnaturally.

The large man wrapped his arms around the limp body. "I'm so sorry, Ed. This should have been me, not you."

Tears streamed down his cheeks onto the top of Ed's crushed skull. The muscular man closed Ed's eyes, zipped his black jacket, and placed Ed's right arm across his bloody chest. He looked around for his brother's hat, and without saying a word, walked over to where it was, picked it up, and brushed the dirt off of the visor. Kneeling beside Ed, the man lifted his younger brother's head and placed the cap on top of it, just like he had when Ed was a little boy going to baseball practice.

The man touched Ed's bloodied hand. "I'll get whoever did this to you. I promise." He riffled through Ed's jacket and pants pockets. "Find it! Now!" he yelled.

Both men knew what he was referring to and combed the blood-covered ground. They pushed the dead bodies aside from their prone positions, searched under cars, and sifted through bushes.

"I found it," the baby-faced man hollered.

The muscular man snatched the device from the young man's hands, examined it, and saw that the red button had been pressed. Fuming, he stood up. "We need to find whoever did this!"

"You got it, Aaron," the tall man said.

Aaron looked down and found tire tracks from the garage leading up to his brother's dead body. He followed the black streaked path to a raised curb by the garage exit. Aaron examined the broken white barrier arm and found blue paint across the top of it. Turning his head in different directions, he caught sight of a blue car smashed head-on into another vehicle. He walked over to it and discovered that the driver's side airbag was covered in blood. He continued around to the front bumper of the car and wedged his fingers between the crashed vehicles. He felt moisture and raised his hand towards the streetlamp, revealing a red liquid. Aaron opened the passenger door, sat in the seat, and pulled the glove compartment open. He took out its contents and rifled through the papers, searching for something specific. He found the car's manual, some oil change receipts, and the document he had been looking for. With the paper in his hand, he moved to the back of the car and verified that the license plate was the same one listed on the registration.

"Get over here!" Aaron yelled.

The two men rushed over to the blue car.

"What's up?" asked the tall man.

"We need to find this guy!" Aaron showed the two men a picture of a man and a woman he had taken from the visor. "He killed my brother!"

"How are we supposed to find him?" the man with the baby face asked.

Aaron turned and walked away. The two men followed him, and they spent the next hour scouring the streets, searching for Ed's killer. They stopped beside a red minivan.

"Look everywhere! I want him found!" Aaron seethed.

"No problem, Aaron," the tall man assured him. "I know finding him's important, but what about the boxes? Should we continue setting them off?"

Crouched behind the minivan, Corey and Isabella stared at each other.

"Did you set yours off?" Aaron asked.

The tall man confirmed he had. "The glass boxes, too."

"I didn't get to all of mine yet," the young man said.

"Why not?" Aaron asked.

"Well, everyone had left the building, and the glass box was empty, so I didn't want to waste them."

Corey looked at Isabella and mouthed, *there's more*?

"How many do you have left?" Aaron asked in disgust.

"I don't know. One? Two? Why does it matter?" the young man scoffed.

"It matters because we're supposed to finish the city and meet at the water station. That's why!" Aaron roared. "Now finish your job, and if you have to move the boxes to different locations, then do it!"

Isabella mouthed to Corey, *Mom*.

"Whatever," the young man grumbled.

Corey and Isabella listened as the men's footsteps faded out of earshot. Corey got down on his stomach and looked under the van to see which way they were heading. One of the men walked in a different direction than the other two, likely the one who hadn't completed his mission. Corey assumed that the other two men were headed to the water station.

After several minutes, Isabella broke the silence. "The water supply? We can't let them do this."

"What about your mother?" Corey asked.

"Maybe they haven't contaminated it yet, and we can try and stop them," Isabella huffed.

"Let's hope. But for now, we'll follow that guy. If we can get him to tell us where the water station is, maybe no one else will have to die."

Isabella hesitated. "Ok. But if it gets out of hand, we stop. I don't want either of us to get hurt."

"Me neither," Corey agreed.

Corey and Isabella snuck along the sidewalk and hid behind a large black truck with *TJ's Landscaping* stenciled in green letters on the passenger side door. The truck was tall enough that it allowed Corey to remain hidden as he looked over the front hood at the young man, crossed the street, and then disappeared between two buildings.

"He went down that alley," Corey whispered. "Stay here. I'll go to the side of that building and wave you over when it's ok."

Corey ran across the street, evading bodies as he went. He squeezed his back against the side of the brick building and peered down the alley. It was littered with newspapers, toppled over garbage cans, broken bottles, and more dead bodies. When the young man reached the end of the alley, Corey waved for Isabella to cross the street.

Isabella stood up, ready to run, but stopped when she heard the other two men's voices. She slid down behind the tire, looked past the back of the truck, and saw them heading in her direction.

Corey also heard the voices and darted behind the driver's side door of a small yellow car. Peeking around the trunk, he saw that the men had stopped in front of the black truck Isabella was hiding behind. Corey squatted with his fists clenched, prepared to fight if necessary.

Isabella's heart raced as the men stood a few feet away from her. She covered her mouth to silence her ragged breathing.

"Go find him and make sure he sets those boxes off. I don't want any more screw-ups."

Isabella recognized this voice; it was Aaron's.

"Sure, no problem. But what if there's nobody around?" the other man asked.

"Bring'm back, and we'll use them outside of the city," Aaron said. "Victor took care of the water supply, so setting off a few more boxes won't hurt. I'll pick you two up later, and remember, if you find this guy Corey, don't kill him. Leave that to me. I want to repay him for what he did to my brother!"

Isabella felt lightheaded, and her stomach twisted in knots. She couldn't swallow. Her eyes became blurry and filled with tears. The voices around her became muted. All she could focus on was the threat of losing Corey.

When Isabella regained her composure, she wasn't sure how much time had passed before she realized that the men had walked away. She glanced around the tire and saw a tall man crossing the street towards Corey. She looked for Corey to warn him, and when she couldn't see him, she panicked. She kneeled on the ground, looked under the truck, and found Corey squatting behind the trunk of the car.

The man reached the other side of the street, sat on the hood of the yellow car, and called out. "Hey, Kevin!"

A voice echoed from the alley. "What?"

The tall man stood up and walked in Kevin's direction, whistling as he went.

Corey waited a few minutes, ran back to the side of the building, and peeked around the corner down the alley. The men had caught up to each other and were talking. Corey waved for Isabella to join him.

Before dashing across the street, Isabella stood up and looked around to make sure Aaron wasn't coming back.

"Did you hear what Aaron said?" Isabella's voice was trembling. "He knows your name!"

Corey took his eyes away from the alley and looked at her in bewilderment, "What do you mean he knows my name? Who?"

"I think the guy we ran over at the garage was Aaron's brother. He said he wants to kill you! Forget about these guys. Let's just go!" Isabella begged, tugging at Corey's injured hand.

"You heard Aaron. They're going outside of the city…"

Isabella interrupted Corey. "He wants to KILL you! Don't you understand?"

"Yes, but we have to try and stop them. What about the water supply? Your mother is in danger."

"They already did something to it, and I can't call my mom to warn her."

Corey placed his hands over Isabella's. "There's nothing we can do for your mother from here. Let's hope she hasn't drunk any of the water."

"Yeah, but what if she has?" Isabella squeezed her eyes shut and shook her head. "I can't think of that!"

Corey wasn't sure of what to say, if anything at all. "We could look for a phone charger in one of these cars, but that could take hours. We could also continue to search for a car to go home, which could take some time as well." Corey pointed to a young woman lying in the middle of the sidewalk. "So for now, let's try to save some people from ending up like her."

Isabella stared at the young woman, who looked to be in her teens. She wore a mauve colored mini-skirt with a white blouse covered in blood and dirt. Her mouth was propped open with a fly sitting on her tongue. Her green eyes, saturated with dried blood, gazed up at Isabella.

"It's your choice. Whatever you decide, we'll do," Corey conceded.

Isabella lowered her head. "I'm scared, Corey."

"Me too. And I want nothing more than to be home with you." Corey hugged Isabella. "But, if we can save one life, then we should do what we can."

"Ok," Isabella conceded.

CHAPTER 12

Corey peered down the alley one more time, and when he didn't see the two men, he and Isabella crept down the dimly lit passageway. With their backs against the building wall, they stepped over tires and bottles, trying not to make a sound. When they reached the end of the street, Corey looked around the corner to make sure the coast was clear.

A loud thunderous *boom* broke the silence.

Isabella grabbed Corey's arm with both hands, digging her nails into his forearm. "What was that?"

"Sounded like a door," Corey whispered.

Corey spotted one of the men walking through the lobby of a building across the street. He tapped Isabella on the thigh and pointed to a grey van.

"We go on three," Corey whispered. "One... two... three."

They ran across the street and slammed their backs against the van.

Corey looked around the taillights and toward the lighted entrance of the building. He turned towards Isabella. "The lobby's empty. I'll run to the door and see if it opens. If it does, I'll wave you on, and we'll go in and to the left, where that desk is." Corey pointed to the brown desk in the lobby.

"Ok," Isabella said.

Corey hurried to the door and yanked on the handle. Without turning around, he heard Isabella's shoes on the concrete steps and held the door open for her. Even amid the chaos, Corey remained a gentleman.

Isabella hurried through the opening and straight to the large security desk covered with a stack of papers, a badge reader, and a computer with the words *Aldridge Building* scrolling across the screen. Next to the computer was a charging station containing four walkie-talkies.

Corey and Isabella heard that unsettling sound of elevator doors opening and crouched behind the desk. Isabella's back was pressed against a black chair, forcing Corey to squeeze his body into the cramped space. The sound of whistling and footsteps echoed through the lobby, followed by the exit door slamming into its metal frame. Corey moved behind Isabella to see which man had left the building and where he was going.

Corey whispered, "Look for something to use as a weapon."

Next to the revolving doors was a tin bucket filled with umbrellas. Across the lobby was a table and chairs, and in front of the elevator doors was a silver trash receptacle.

Isabella tapped Corey on the shoulder and pointed to an area under the stairs. There were four gold metal stanchions with retractable belts, the kind used to rope off guests at a movie theater.

"I'll run over and grab one. You keep an eye out for him," Corey said.

Corey stood halfway up, took one last glance at the door, and ran across the open space. He grabbed a gold stanchion, then made his way back to the desk. Isabella removed the plastic cover from the metal bar and ripped the belt out of the spring mechanism, while Corey unscrewed the pole from the circular base.

A gust of wind swirled through the lobby, followed by whistling again. Corey paid close attention to the tall skinny man walking across the marble floor, making sure that he wasn't coming their way. The dull echo of footsteps fell silent as the man entered the elevator. The door closed, and soon after, Corey and Isabella heard a ding.

"Follow me," Corey instructed.

Pole in hand, Corey ran across the lobby to the elevators. Isabella was right behind him, holding the strap. They watched each number light up above the door frame until it stopped on the eleventh floor.

"Quick. The stairs," Corey directed.

They sprinted through the elevator lobby to the fire exit door and into the stairwell. Corey took two steps at a time while Isabella tried to keep pace with him. When they reached the tenth floor, they stopped to catch their breath, gasping for air. After a minute, they snuck up the last twelve steps to the eleventh floor.

Corey cracked the exit door open just enough for a beam of light to protrude into the dark stairwell. He pressed his ear to the cold metal but couldn't hear a thing. He pulled open the door enough so that his head fit through, and to his left was a wall; to his right was an empty corridor.

"Stay here. I want to check the hallway," Corey said.

"No," Isabella whispered. "We do this together, or we don't do it at all." Isabella was very adamant about her decision and would not be deterred.

Corey nodded in agreement, and with the stanchion pole in his hand, he stepped into the corridor with Isabella by his side. He used his injured hand to guide his path along the wall until they reached the elevator lobby. Corey tilted his head around the corner, but no one was there. They continued their stealthy movement across the open lobby as if they had stumbled upon a lion's den filled with sleeping predators. Halfway down the hall, they reached an office with its lights on. Corey peered through the door's entrance but didn't see any movement, so they continued down the hallway.

Corey and Isabella reached the end of the corridor with no sign of either of the men. They turned around to head back but stopped when they spotted a heavyset man coming out of the office with the lights on. Corey could feel Isabella's heart thumping against his back and put his hand on her waist, signaling her to stop moving.

The husky man wore a dark blue business suit, with a white shirt peeking out from under his jacket, and carried a brown leather briefcase. With his back toward Corey and Isabella, the man closed the door and took a set of keys from his pocket. In an attempt to lock the door, the man dropped his keys.

Corey heard Isabella gasp and pressed his body into hers. They watched as the man picked the keys up, locked the office door, and walked down the hallway toward the elevators.

A ding rang out, and then voices could be heard.

"Can I help you, gentlemen?" a male voice inquired.

"Uhm, sure," a different male voice responded.

Corey and Isabella knew this voice. It was the tall man that they had heard from earlier.

There was a *thud*, a groan, and then a louder *thud*.

The man from the office had fallen, and part of his body was visibly lying in the hallway where Corey and Isabella stood. They could see blood seeping down the side of his head onto the carpet. As they stood motionless, the man's body was dragged along the floor.

"Hey, come help me! He's a heavy sucker," the tall man quipped. "He's still breathing. Let's put him in the room."

When the young man came into view, Corey backed up, squishing Isabella into the corner of the hallway, hiding her from sight. Corey could feel her hot breath on his neck.

The young man hooked his arms under the large man's shoulders, picked up the top half of his body, lumbered forward, and vanished out of sight.

Corey whispered, "We need to follow them to see where they're going."

"No! They just killed that man. We have to leave," Isabella protested.

"They said he's still breathing."

"You said if it gets too dangerous, we leave."

"Ok. But we need to know where they are first, so we don't get caught."

Corey and Isabella walked down the hallway sticking as close as possible to the wall and each other. Upon reaching the end of the hall, Corey saw blood on the carpet and the man's briefcase next to one of his polished black shoes. Corey tiptoed into the elevator lobby with the pole in his hand, while Isabella followed with the strap in hers. They stopped at the end of the wall, and Corey poked his head around the corner just in time to witness the two men drop the man's body on the floor.

"You put him in the room. I'm gonna get his briefcase," the tall man directed.

"Look at that? He pissed himself." The young man laughed as he walked around the body. He picked up the man's feet and pulled him into an office, banging the man's head against the wall as he went.

Corey jerked his head back. He took Isabella's hand and tugged her back into the hallway they just came from. While pressed against the wall, Corey's breathing became short and shallow, and he had a hard time swallowing. Adrenaline coursed through his veins, temporarily disguising the pain radiating in his injured hand. He peeked around the corner, squeezed the metal cylinder with both hands, and played the scenario out in his head.

The tall man turned the corner and picked up the briefcase laying on the ground. He examined it, then pressed the two square buttons to the sides, but it wouldn't open. In anger, he threw it up against the wall, unsuccessfully breaking the lock. He pulled a switchblade out of his pocket, kneeled, and pried one of the locks open.

Before the man had the chance to pry the other lock open, something dripped down his forehead and into his eye. He attempted to stand but fell back to his knees, bracing himself with his hand. He put his fingers on top of his head and then stared at the blood covering them. "What the hell?"

The delayed feeling of pain caught up to him, and his skull started to ache. He moaned, then closed his eyes and dropped his head. He blindly reached forward and put his bloody hand on the wall in front of him. He staggered to his feet but lost his balance and fell backward into the wall.

Corey snapped out of his daze and found himself in the middle of the elevator lobby, the metal stanchion held high above his head.

The tall man opened his eyes. "Who are…"

Corey swung the pole down onto the side of the man's face with a loud *crack*. The man's eyes rolled into the back of his head, and he slid down the wall onto the carpet. Corey raised the metal pole again and then felt a hand on his forearm. He turned his upper body so fast that his elbow struck something on the way by.

Isabella stood in front of him, holding the top of her head. "I think he's dead."

Corey dropped the bloody pole, and it fell onto the dead man's back, then rolled onto the ground. Corey's chest tightened, and he couldn't catch his breath. His face turned ghost-white, and he ran over to a corner of the lobby and threw up. Wiping his mouth with the sleeve of his jacket, Corey looked back at Isabella. "I'm so sorry. Are you ok?"

"I'm fine," she said.

"What…have I done?"

"You did what you had to do to save us."

Isabella walked over to Corey, took his arms, put them around her waist, and then placed her arms around his neck. She could feel the rhythm of his heartbeat slowing down. She put her hands on Corey's cheeks and pressed her forehead to his.

"We have to leave. The other guy could be coming down the hall any second," stated Isabella.

Corey looked down at the dead man covered in blood. "No. We have to finish this," he said in a robotic tone.

Isabella took Corey's hand and guided him to the corner of the lobby wall. She peeked down the corridor and saw that it was empty. She glanced back at Corey, noticing that his eyes were glazed over, and he was staring into space.

"Are you ready?" she asked.

"I…I just need a minute," he replied.

After Corey had composed himself, they crept down the corridor toward the office where the young man had entered.

Isabella turned toward Corey. "Are you able to do this?" she asked with concern in her tone.

"I think so."

Corey inched in front of Isabella so he could see into the office. The young man was not in sight, but the heavyset man in the blue suit was lying in the middle of the office floor, with his face covered in blood and a large purple bump on top of his bald head.

"I don't see him. I need to go in and find him." Corey's voice was steadier.

"You can't go in there by yourself." Isabella showed Corey the belt she had taken from the top of the gold stanchion.

"He's young and small. I'll get him to the ground, and you tie him up. Wait for me to call you in." Corey looked at Isabella, making sure she understood what he had just said. "Not a minute before!"

"Be careful," she emphasized.

Corey walked through the open door into the office lobby and looked down at the dead man, whose eyes were still open. Corey leaned over and closed them.

"Hey! What are you doing here?" a voice called out from behind Corey.

CHAPTER 13

Corey, startled by the voice, glanced over his shoulder and saw the young man sitting behind the reception desk. Corey stood up and turned in the man's direction.

"Kevin, right? That's your name, isn't it?" Corey asked, trying to gain control of the situation before it got out of hand.

"How do you know my name?" Kevin got up from the chair and advanced toward Corey. "Where's Dean?"

Corey stepped back towards the opening of the door. "I just spoke to him. He said you'd be in here."

"Who are you?" Kevin continued moving forward.

With his hands by his side, Corey wiggled his fingers at Isabella, instructing her to back up from the door so she wouldn't be seen. "Like I said, Dean sent me in here."

Kevin lunged at Corey, pushing him over the body on the ground. Corey's back hit the floor, knocking the wind out of him. Isabella screamed. Kevin looked in her direction and charged at her.

Corey reached across the dead man's chest and grabbed Kevin's ankle, knocking him off balance. Kevin fell forward to the ground but was able to brace himself with his hands. As Corey got up, Kevin kicked him in the chest, propelling him back into the wall. Kevin got to his feet and rushed at Corey, who reacted by throwing a punch at Kevin's face. Kevin ducked and countered with a jab to Corey's ribs. Kevin followed up with a straight punch to Corey's face, but at the last possible second, Corey saw it, shifted his head out of the way, and Kevin's fist struck the wall. The crunch of bones breaking rang in Corey's ear. Kevin grabbed his hand and cried out in agony.

Corey stepped between Kevin's legs, leaned his shoulder into his stomach, wrapped his arms around Kevin's lower back, and drove him backward into the reception desk. Kevin planted his feet firmly on the floor and came down with an elbow to the center of Corey's spine, forcing Corey to the ground. Kevin lifted his knee into Corey's face, striking his nose, spraying blood over Corey's lips and into his mouth. Corey collapsed onto the carpeted floor in the middle of the reception area.

Kevin smirked at Corey and then reached into his jacket pocket. Corey knew what Kevin was trying to get, so he rushed at him and grabbed Kevin's wrist. Corey balled up his injured right hand and threw it at Kevin, connecting to the side of his cheek. Kevin's head snapped to the right, with so much force that they both toppled over to the ground. Corey landed on top of Kevin's chest, with his hand still clutched in a vice-like grip to Kevin's wrist.

Pinning Kevin to the ground with his body, Corey demanded, "Why are you doing this?"

Kevin took his injured hand, grabbed a tuft of Corey's hair, and yanked him over the side of his body. He rolled on top of Corey and began a barrage of downward punches. Corey covered his face with his arms, but some of the strikes got through, hitting him in the nose and cheeks.

Corey heard Isabella scream and peeked through his arms to see that she was on Kevin's back, with her legs wrapped around his waist and the strap around his neck.

Kevin stood up, reached over his shoulder, grabbed the corner of Isabella's jacket, and pulled her over his head, flinging her to the ground with a *thud*. Kevin reached into his pocket and pulled out a black device. He held it high in the air for them to see, then backed up towards the office exit and pressed the button.

Like a roller coaster climbing up its first hill, mechanical clicking sounds roared through the office. Corey and Isabella watched as sheets of glass inched down the four walls and across the ceiling. Another pane of glass crept down from the ceiling, in front of the wooden office door.

They looked at each other. "Glass box!"

Corey stood up, ran through the exit door, and crashed into Kevin, launching him into the air and dislodging the black device from his hand. Just as Kevin landed on the carpet with a *thump*, Corey was on him, punching and kneeing Kevin's body, ignoring the searing pain radiating through his injured hand.

Isabella wobbled to her feet, like a newborn calf. She watched in terror as the glass descended past the half-way point on the walls giving her a sense of claustrophobia. When she regained her balance, she bounded through the doorway past Corey and Kevin.

Slight as he was, Kevin was much stronger than Corey had anticipated. As the two men wrestled against the outside wall of the office, Corey grabbed the lapels of Kevin's jacket, placed a foot behind one of Kevin's legs, and pushed him across the door's threshold. Corey lost his balance and crashed down on top of Kevin.

Boom!

The four glass walls slammed into the floor, and locking mechanisms clicked. The sound startled Corey, and he looked into the office. Kevin took advantage of this distraction and kneed Corey in the groin. Corey winced in pain and curled into a fetal position with his hands clasped between his thighs. Corey's body was lying across the entrance of the door, and he would be crushed if he didn't move.

Something switched inside Isabella. Her body tensed, and the hair on the back of her neck stood up. Noises turned to whispers, and movements seemed to slow down. The glass door continued to drop like sand in an hourglass. With little regard for her safety, Isabella ran to Corey, grabbed his ankles, and yanked him out from under the descending sheet of glass. She turned toward Kevin just in time to see him reaching for her. Instinctively she fell to the ground on her hands and knees, forming a bridge with her back. Kevin plummeted him over her and fell in front of the descending glass door. Isabella rolled onto her back, recoiled her knees into her chest, and with all of her strength, she used the bottom of her feet to thrust Kevin's body into the middle of the office floor.

Boom!

The glass door slammed down into the floor, and a locking mechanism clicked.

Isabella clambered to her feet, stood in front of the glass door, and locked eyes with Kevin. Slowly she raised her hand, revealing the black device, then pressed the red button.

"Nooooo!" Kevin punched the glass with his fist.

Kevin ran back into the office, grabbed a chair, and threw it at the glass door. It bounced back and landed upside down on the carpet. He threw a table, then another chair, and in a last-ditch effort, he threw himself. He opened his mouth as if to saying something, but instead, he grabbed his throat with both hands. He staggered around the office lobby and tripped over the man on the floor. Kevin's head shook back and forth while specks of foam propelled from his mouth. He got to his feet and ran towards the door, slamming his body against the glass.

Corey flinched, but Isabella didn't move. She stood transfixed, devoid of remorse. Corey nudged her with his elbow, but she remained unresponsive. He called her name, but she didn't answer. She simply watched.

Kevin's face was covered with so much blood that he was unrecognizable. The whites of his eyes rolled into the back of his head, and his hands moved down to the sides of his body with his thumbs pointing at his thighs. He fell backward.

Isabella dropped the device from her hand. It landed at her feet, toppled over, and stopped in front of the glass door.

Corey placed his hands on her shoulders and turned her towards him. "Are you ok?"

Isabella nodded her head, yes. "That could have been us." She buried her head into Corey's chest. "I want to go home."

Corey wrapped his arm around her shoulder, and they headed down the hall. When they reached the elevator lobby, they looked down at the dead man.

"We've done some unthinkable things tonight." Isabella paused, "But I would do it again if it meant saving you."

"I would too." Corey leaned in and kissed her cheek.

They took the elevator down to the first floor.

Corey stepped out into the lobby and stopped. "Do you hear that?"

"Hear what?" Isabella turned her head in different directions, listening for a specific sound.

"That's just it. I don't hear anything. No people. No sirens. I don't even hear the wind outside." Corey moved forward across the lobby.

"Where are you going?" Isabella asked.

Without turning around, Corey said, "Stay there. I want to make sure that it's safe outside."

Corey reached the exit door and pushed the horizontal metal bar with his hip. Brisk air swept over him as he stepped into the night. He braced the door open with his foot and swiveled his head around to make sure the coast was clear. He turned back toward Isabella and motioned for her to join him.

The bright light, overhead in the lobby, illuminated Corey's dimples and sparkling blue eyes. Isabella smiled, closed her eyes, and took a deep sigh of relief. When she opened her eyes, her smile disappeared, and her feeling of comfort turned into fear. She attempted to speak, but nothing came out of her mouth. She tried to run forward, but her legs wouldn't move. She couldn't even lift her arms to point.

Corey recognized the look of fear on her face. His dimples disappeared, his eyes widened, and pain rushed through his body. At first, he thought the pain had to do with his wrist, but then his head began to ache, and his eyesight became blurry. He staggered back with dizziness and plummeted forward onto the cement. The lobby door swung shut with a quiet *whoosh*.

Isabella watched as a large man picked Corey up and tossed him over his shoulder. The light from the full moon revealed the attacker's face…it was Aaron!

Aaron descended the cement stairs and flung Corey into the back of a white pickup truck. He turned, looked back at Isabella, and waved.

When Isabella snapped out of her state of shock, she ran across the lobby and barreled through the exit door, shoulder first. As she reached the concrete stairs, Aaron sped off, leaving a cloud of smoke in its wake. She ran after the vehicle shouting Corey's name. Her chest tightened, and the world around her darkened. She collapsed to the ground, sobbing. The truck drove further and further away until it disappeared out of sight.

CHAPTER 14

Aaron looked in his rearview mirror and watched the girl fall to her knees in the middle of the street. He chuckled to himself, then pulled Corey's registration from his shirt pocket and entered the address on it into the truck's GPS.

After thirty minutes, Aaron approached his destination. He turned off the headlights and drove down the long dirt road, spitting small pebbles from beneath the tires. Floodlights from the house exposed a portion of the gravel road forcing Aaron to pull the front of the truck onto the lawn. He turned off the engine, open the driver's side door, stepped onto the dew-covered grass, and marched to the back of the truck. When Aaron opened the tailgate, he noticed that Corey had rolled into the truck's sidewall and blood smeared across the bed liner.

"Damn it. You got blood on my truck." Aaron shoved Corey's feet aside and grabbed a quarter piece of campfire wood.

Corey lay motionless, not wanting Aaron to find out that he had regained consciousness. The sound of Aaron's footsteps on the gravel road faded as he walked away from the truck. Corey lifted his head high enough to catch a glimpse of his surroundings. His body stiffened when he realized that Aaron had taken him to Isabella's house.

While he watched Aaron veer toward the side of the house, Corey touched the top of his head and felt stickiness in his hair. Blood had clotted on his scalp and down the back of his neck. He put his other hand on the side of the truck and forced himself to his knees. Corey looked toward the front porch, and when he couldn't see Aaron anymore, he swung his leg over the side of the truck and maneuvered his body onto the ledge. As he picked up his other leg, he lost his grip and tumbled to the ground. He landed on his back, expelling air from his mouth in an audible gasp. Hoping Aaron didn't see or hear him, Corey rolled over the small but singularly sharp pebbles under the truck. He could feel heat on his back from the undercarriage.

Corey focused his gaze in the direction of the house as he crawled onto the wet grass. He staggered to his feet and leaned against the nearest tree, taking a few seconds to catch his breath. He searched the surrounding area, and when he didn't see Aaron, he careened off trees until he reached his destination, a trench of water surrounding the property.

Corey stepped into the ditch, and water filled his shoes and soaked through his clothes onto his skin. He peered up over the two-foot-tall wall of dirt just in time to witness Aaron sneaking around to the back of the house.

Aaron came across a small porch with a door and a window covered by a floral curtain from the inside. As he climbed the wooden steps, his body twitched with each nerve-racking creak. He put his hand on the doorknob and turned it clockwise, but it wouldn't go any further. He turned it counterclockwise, and again, it stopped. Not wanting to make any more noise, he leaped over the three steps onto the plush lawn. He continued around to the other side of the house and found an open window. He stood on the balls of his feet, peeked through the screen, and observed a woman kneeling next to her bed, her hands clasped in prayer. He ducked his head below the window frame and continued his reconnaissance of the property.

Aaron crept further along the side of the house and discovered a bulkhead door. He lifted the metal handle, but the door wouldn't budge. He continued around to the front of the house, where two white rocking chairs sat on the porch, one of which was gliding back and forth as if a ghost were sitting in it. He put his foot on the first wooden step, and it creaked just like the back steps had. He moved his foot to the edge of the step and pressed down in silence. When the second step was quiet, he placed his foot over the last step onto the porch. He peered through the screen door, down a hallway, and into a kitchen. Reaching for the rusted handle, a shadow appeared from the room on the right, just past the stairs, followed by footsteps and a woman's voice.

"Isabella, is that you?"

Aaron slid to the left side of the screen door, placed his back against the siding of the house, and raised the log above his head. The screen door opened, and the woman stepped onto the porch. She walked to the top step, looked across the yard, and called out.

"Isabella!"

Aaron kept a careful eye on the woman as she stood there with her arms folded across her chest. When no one answered her call, Aaron took a step toward her. The woman turned, and before she could scream, Aaron brought the piece of wood down on the top of her head. The woman collapsed and tumbled down the stairs into a puddle of mud. Aaron vaulted over the steps and landed next to the woman, the bloody log dangling by his side.

Aaron picked her up, carried her into the house, and dropped her onto the living room floor. He grabbed a chair from the kitchen and brought it into the hallway, placing it in front of the living room. He returned to the kitchen, rummaged through several drawers finding a spindle of twine, a roll of duct tape, and a pair of scissors. He returned to the living room and placed the items on a coffee table next to a plate and a glass of water.

After Aaron had cut several pieces of twine, he lifted the woman under her arms, dragged her across the carpet, and sat her in the chair. He tilted the woman's chin up to let her head hang over the back of the chair. He moved her arms by her sides and placed her feet in front of the chair to steady her wilting body. He tied her ankles to the chair legs and bound her hands together behind her back. He wrapped the longer piece of twine around her waist, pulled it tight around the back of the chair, and knotted it. He took the duct tape, cut a small piece, and placed it over the woman's mouth. Finally, he dragged the chair closer to the front door and turned it so that the woman faced the front porch.

Aaron exited through the screen porch door and let it slam back into the frame. The twang of the springs echoed in the night as the door bounced off the wood. He walked to the back of his truck, put his hand on the tailgate latch, and discovered that Corey was missing. Aaron gritted his teeth in rage, swung his head in all directions, and bellowed, "Where are you?"

Aaron discovered a bloody handprint on the side of the truck. He kneeled on the ground and found a trail of blood leading under the cab, across the dirt road. He stormed around to the driver's side and followed the dark stain to the wet grass, but the trail ended there. "I'll find you!" he shouted.

Despite the brightness from the full moon, Aaron had difficulty searching for Corey through the grove of trees. In his exploration, a glimmer of light appeared, and a car door slammed shut. He ran back to the front of his truck and hid behind the grill. He looked up the driveway to see who was approaching and could only make out a shadowy figure carrying something thin in one of their hands. *It can't be that girl,* he thought to himself.

CHAPTER 15

Isabella stumbled to her feet, her knees drenched in blood and the palms of her hands peppered with tiny piercing stones. Her hair was splayed over her shoulders, and a spider web of dried tears covered the film of dirt on her cheeks. She stood in the middle of the abandoned intersection, wondering where Aaron had taken Corey and how Aaron had known it was Corey who killed his brother. She closed her eyes and tried to visualize being back behind the minivan. She replayed what Aaron had said to the other men after mentioning Corey's name.

"I'll pick you two up later and remember, if you find this guy Corey, don't kill him. Leave that to me. I want to repay him for what he did to my brother!"

Isabella couldn't remember anything else. She paced in the street, growing angrier with herself for having not paid attention at the time. She stopped, closed her eyes again, and placed her hands over her ears, drowning out the background noise of distant sirens and car alarms.

"What are you going to do with him?" a man had asked.

"I got his car registration. I'll be going there."

Isabella's eyes snapped open. "Mom!"

She glanced around the immediate area and located an unoccupied gray car. She rushed over to the driver's side door, opened it, and searched for car keys, with no luck. She tried several other empty vehicles, but none of them contained keys. She resigned herself to the fact that she would have to find a vehicle, not only with keys in the ignition but also likely to have a body inside.

Isabella picked out a Ford Explorer, and, through the open window, she could see a woman inside covered in foam and blood with her dead eyes affixed to the rearview mirror. In the backseat was a little boy, who couldn't have been more than five, wearing a baseball cap sitting in a car seat. His green eyes were wide, and streaks of blood ran down his cheeks onto his t-shirt, imprinted with a picture of Optimus Prime. His head was tilted up, looking over the back of the driver's seat toward his mother. Isabella didn't have the heart to remove them from the Explorer and abandon them on the sidewalk as if they were garbage.

Isabella noticed the woman's purse and cell phone on the passenger seat. She rushed around to the other side of the SUV, opened the door, and picked up the phone. She pressed the power button, and the screen brightened, but it required a passcode to use it. She moved the purse to the floor and sat in the passenger seat. She lifted the woman's thumb and pressed it to the circle on the bottom of the phone, but nothing happened. She did the same thing with the woman's index finger, and the screen came alive, showing icons on the display. She dialed her mother's cell phone, but there was no answer, so she left a voice mail.

"Hi, Mom, it's me. Cory was kidnapped by some guy, and I…I think he's heading to the house. Call the police. I'm trying to find a car to get home. I'll be there as soon as I can. Call me on this number when you get this message." Isabella was about to hang up when she remembered the water. "Oh yeah, some guys did something to the city water. I don't know what, but don't use it." Isabella hung up the phone, put it in her coat, and then continued her frantic search for a vehicle.

She approached a black Chevy Blazer and opened the driver's side door revealing a young man, perhaps in his twenties, wearing a white collared shirt with a pastel blue tie. Isabella tore off a piece of cloth from the bottom of her dress and wrapped it around her nose and mouth. She reached over the man's body and unbuckled his seat belt. She opened the driver's side passenger door, took the man's suit coat off a hanger, wrapped it around his arm, and pulled until his whole body tumbled into the street. Isabella pressed the rear hatch button, walked around to the back of the truck, and found a red Nebraska Cornhuskers blanket. She folded it and placed it on the blood-stained driver's seat. She removed the mask from her face, got into the truck, and started the truck's engine. When the navigational system appeared in a small LED window above the heating vents, she entered her home address, shifted the Blazer into drive, and sped off.

Isabella slalomed through the unfamiliar city streets, scattered with upturned vehicles, dead bodies, and people wandering about. Trucks had crashed into telephone poles, while abandoned police cars continued to flash their red and blue lights. Isabella made every attempt to avoid running over bodies, but against her best intentions, she heard what sounded like the crunching of celery under the tires.

Isabella slammed on the brakes, and the car halted to a stop in front of Corey's office building. She put the truck in park, ran over to Corey's abandoned car, and searched the front and back seats. When she didn't find what she was looking for, she ran around to the opened trunk. She took the flashlight from the open roadside kit, then lifted the trunk's carpeted flooring, revealing a spare tire and the item she had been searching for, a crowbar. She ran back to the Blazer and zoomed down the street.

Isabella's mind wandered as she drove through the streets, following the verbal commands of the GPS navigation system. She tried not to imagine what would happen to her mom if Aaron found her. What about Corey? Was he still alive? Her anxiety rose with each frightening thought, causing her to lose focus on the road. She took a right turn, and a man appeared in front of her truck. She stomped on the brake pedal with both feet, and the tires screeched while smoke billowed from the rubber tires. She stopped inches in from a man, but the inertia of her body propelled her forward into the steering wheel. She rebounded back into the cloth seat behind her, and her head thumped into the headrest. She looked through the windshield and prayed that she hadn't hit the man. But, there he stood, eyes wide, mouth open, and his hands high in the air like he was just robbed.

Isabella poked her head out of the car window. "Sorry. Are you ok?"

The man stood frozen, staring at her. He looked distraught, with his shirt torn at the shoulder and his hair disheveled. He slammed the palms of his hands on the hood of her truck and then, without warning, sprinted to the driver's side.

Isabella pressed the button to raise her window, but she wasn't quick enough. The man placed both of his hands on top of the glass and pressed downward, preventing the window from rising. He leaned in toward Isabella and shouted obscenities at her. She could smell his stale breath wafting in her face, and it took everything she had not to vomit.

Isabella panicked and pressed the gas pedal, hoping the man would let go, but he didn't. He ran alongside the truck as it drove down the street. With a clawed hand, the man reached inside the car window toward Isabella's throat. She screamed and jolted her head away from his fingers.

Isabella could feel the truck picking up speed and saw that the speedometer glowed the number twenty-two. The man held onto the window, but he wasn't running anymore; he was being dragged. Isabella swerved left, then right, crossing the double yellow line in the middle of the street. Glaring out of the front windshield, Isabella saw a parked car on the left side of the road. She veered the truck towards it, and when she was close enough, she stepped on the gas pedal and swerved hard into the parked car.

The Blazer's headlight grazed the driver's side quarter panel and smashed through the parked car's mirror. The man's lower body hit the car's headlights and his legs dragged across the front hood onto the windshield. Isabella heard a thump as the man's body tumbled across the top of the roof and down the back windshield onto the trunk. She glanced back in her side mirror and watched the man roll off the car and onto the pavement. His body flopped on the ground, and his arms flailed until he came to a stop.

Isabella shifted her eyes back onto the road in front of her and saw a sign for the interstate. She drifted the truck onto the on-ramp and raced down the three-lane highway, passing abandoned vehicles on the shoulder of the road. Her hands gripped the steering wheel tight enough that the whites of her knuckles reflected off the front windshield. The GPS indicated that she would reach her destination in fifteen minutes.

Isabella exited the highway faster than she had planned to. The Blazer's back end slid to one side of the road, and Isabella turned the steering wheel in the opposite direction to counteract the slide. The truck jumped over the curb, onto the grass, and slammed into a stop sign at the end of the ramp. Her head thrust forward, whacking her mouth on top of the steering wheel and splitting her lower lip, sending the taste of salt across her tongue. The sound of a creaking door filled the air as the stop sign collapsed onto the hood of the truck. Steam exploded from the grill, and a light mist sprayed the windshield while the engine sputtered to a stop.

Isabella slammed the palms of her hands onto the steering wheel. "Damn it!"

The steam from the hood dissipated, and the water on the windshield dripped down, creating vertical streaks of visibility. Isabella turned the windshield wipers on, and she saw the stop sign had impaled the front hood. She exited the truck, dislodged the sign, and threw it on the ground. Returning to the truck, she turned the ignition key, but the engine wouldn't start.

"C'mon, start," Isabella pleaded.

She tried the engine again, and this time it started right up. She put the truck in drive, drove off the grass, and down the street. She slowed down as she approached a red light at an intersection. She looked around for other cars on the road, and when she didn't see any, she zoomed through it.

As she got closer to home, vivid images of Corey being tied up and beaten flashed in her mind. "Aaron must be there by now," she muttered under her breath.

Isabella pulled over to the side of the road just before her house and turned off the truck's headlights and engine. She grabbed the crowbar and flashlight from the passenger seat, stepped onto the road, and closed the door with her hip.

The brightness of the full moon illuminated the gravel road in front of Isabella's house, and it also revealed the white truck. Isabella snuck toward her house, hiding behind clumps of trees as she went. When she reached the trench surrounding the farm, she stepped over the gap but lost her balance and fell backward into the water. Before she could do anything, her mouth was stifled by a hand. Isabella flailed her arms and legs, but another arm and set of legs wrapped around her body. She was trapped!

Hot breath touched her ear, and she heard a whisper. "It's me, Corey."

Stunned, Isabella was filled with a sudden sense of relief, which allowed her to relax her arms and legs. She dropped the crowbar in the water, and the back of her head rested on Corey's chest. She could feel his heart pounding on the back of her skull. When Corey removed his hand from over her mouth, she rolled over onto her stomach and wept, muffling the sound against his chest.

Corey tightened his arms around Isabella. "Are you ok?"

She didn't answer; she just kissed him. Tears dripped from her cheeks onto his. She wiggled her arms under his shoulder blades and could feel the gritty water on his jacket.

"I'm so happy to see you," she whispered. "Are *you* ok?"

"Yeah, I'm fine. Just a headache to go with my injured hand and bloody forehead."

"Do you know where my mom is?" Isabella asked.

Corey shook his head. "No."

Isabella got to her knees and felt the water seeping through her dress. She put her hands on top of the trench and used the moonlight to see if Aaron was still by his truck.

"His truck's empty," she said.

"I know." Corey got to his knees beside Isabella. "He wasn't around when I woke up, so I got out of the truck as fast as I could and ran down here."

"Do you think he's in the house?"

"I don't think so," Corey answered. "I watched him walk over to his truck just before you showed up."

"Then he still might be out here searching for us. We need to get to my mom before he does!" Isabella started to get up.

Corey put his hand on Isabella's shoulder. "Wait. We can't see him. He could be hiding behind a tree with a weapon or something. We can go along the trench to the back of your house and use your hidden key to sneak in the back door."

"Ok." Isabella fished through the water with her hand.

"What are you looking for?"

Isabella ignored him and continued her exploration. She lifted the crowbar out of the water and handed it to Corey. "I got this from your trunk."

"Good thinking," Corey remarked.

As they waded through the muddy trench on their hands and knees, the tips of Isabella's blonde hair grazed the top of the water. She felt a tap on her lower back and turned to see Corey holding a string from his shoe. She smiled, stopped, and tied her hair into a ponytail. Even living through this nightmare, Corey was always thinking of her.

They continued their approach around the trench, noticing that the moonlight cast a dark shadow over the house, blocking the view of the back porch. Isabella stood up, pulled the flashlight from her pocket, aimed it downward in the trench, and switched it on. The sight of what they had been crawling in made Isabella gasp! The murky water surrounding their legs was covered with hundreds of dead insects floating on top. The mud-wall lining was studded with earthworms, wiggling their bodies in mid-air, while millipedes and beetles unsuccessfully crawled up the embankments.

Isabella's white dress, which hung below her knees, was covered in sludgy brown water. A common water snake brushed against her calf, and she covered her mouth to stifle her scream. A four-legged water strider climbed up Corey's forearm, and he brushed it off nonchalantly. Isabella climbed out of the trench, dropped the flashlight, and shook her body to free herself from the bugs clinging to her. She jiggled her hands and each foot while shrugging her shoulders and shaking her head side to side.

Corey climbed out of the trench, switched off the flashlight lying, and whisked away worms and dirt from his jacket and pants. "We need to go," he urged.

After Isabella had stopped shuddering around, Corey aimed the flashlight at the ground and switched it back on. They tiptoed to the stairs in the back of the house. Corey lifted the flowerpot and took the spare house key from under it.

Having lived in this house her entire life and sneaking out on occasions, Isabella knew how to avoid the parts of each step that creaked. She stepped on the far left of the first step, then the middle of the second step, but when she stepped over the last step onto the center of the porch, she lost her balance. Corey's hand appeared out of nowhere against her back, preventing her from falling.

When both of her feet were firmly in place on the porch, Isabella shuffled her body to the right, then stepped each foot in an intricate pattern leading to the door, as if she were playing a modified game of Twister. She looked through the pane of glass into the empty kitchen and saw that the utility drawer had been opened. As her eyes scoured the kitchen, she waved to Corey to join her on the porch.

When Corey stood next to Isabella, he could feel the negative energy radiating from her rigid body. Her nose and the palms of her hands were pressed against the glass, and her breath created a circle of fog. Corey peered into the kitchen but only saw an open drawer. The longer he stared, the more focused his view became, and he realized what had caused Isabella to freeze. Her mother was seated in a chair in the hallway, not moving.

Isabella reached for the doorknob but was stopped when Corey put his hand on top of hers. "What if he's in there?" he questioned.

"I don't care. That's my mom!"

"You're no good to her if you're dead."

Corey inserted the key into the lock, unlocked the door, and slowly turned the doorknob, listening for the latch assembly to disengage from the strike plate. When it did, he eased the door open and listened for footsteps or a voice. It was silent, so he opened the door enough to step inside. He motioned with his hand for Isabella to stay where she was.

With the crowbar in hand, Corey stepped around the kitchen table towards the hallway. He listened again for noises, but uncomfortable silence echoed in his ears. He stared at Mrs. McCormick, propped up like a doll on a shelf, with her head tilted over the back of the chair and her body slumped to the right as if she were about to fall. Her arms, legs, and waist were bound with a thin rope, and blood had dried on the side of her face. Corey felt a sense of relief when he saw her shoulders moving up and down, indicating that she was still alive. But for how long? Corey had to do something, quick.

Corey looked around the kitchen for something to cut the ropes. He found a wooden knife block just above the open kitchen drawer. He peeked around the corner at Mrs. McCormick, and without hesitation, he reached across the open doorway and pulled a knife from its slot. It wasn't the longest knife, but it was something. He turned back toward Isabella, who was now standing in the kitchen, next to the opened door.

Isabella closed the door and crept next to Corey. "I want to see my mom," she urged.

Corey maneuvered behind her and put his hand on her shoulder as she peeked around the corner. She put her hand to her mouth and turned towards Corey.

"She'll be ok. I'll cut her loose," Corey assured her.

"Is she dead?" Isabella's voice quivered.

"No, but we need to cut her loose before Aaron gets back. Hold this."

Corey handed the crowbar to Isabella, got on his hands and knees, and crawled on the wooden floor toward the back of the chair. When he reached the living room's entryway, he looked around the corner and saw a spindle of twine, duct tape, scissors, a plate, and a glass of water sitting on the living room table. He continued crawling along the floor, and when he reached the back of the chair, he touched Mrs. McCormick's calf, feeling the warmth of her body.

Corey cut the twine from Mrs. McCormick's ankles, hands, and waist. Her arms dropped down by her sides, revealing deep rope burns on her wrists. Corey put the knife on the floor and peered over the chair's bottom rungs through the screen porch door. A large shape was approaching from the front lawn. Corey looked back at Isabella, who was waving for him to return. He crawled backward on his stomach, into the kitchen, and around the corner. He got to his feet and took the crowbar from Isabella.

CHAPTER 16

Footsteps stomped up the front porch stairs, shaking the house. The hinges squeaked as the screen door was yanked open. A deep, angry voice bellowed throughout the house.

"Where the hell are you, Corey?"

Isabella edged closer to Corey, placing her trembling hands on his back. He held the crowbar high above his head, waiting for Aaron to come around the corner.

"You cut the ropes. Smart kid. But you forgot one thing," Aaron sneered.

Corey knew what he had forgotten, the knife. He gritted his teeth and shook his head in disgust.

Aaron leaned down and picked up the weapon. The moonlight, streaming through the front door, reflected off the blade and onto his face, revealing his anger and murderous intent. "You took my brother from me! Now I'm going to take something from you!" Aaron barked.

Corey peeked into the hallway and watched as Aaron plunged the knife into Mrs. McCormick's abdomen. She moaned through the duct tape, and her body twitched while her hands and feet convulsed forward and her head dropped down to her chest.

Aaron stared down at her limp body, slumped over in the chair, and raised the knife again.

Corey's body shook, and the crowbar felt heavier in his trembling hands. Adrenaline surged through him, and he charged into the hallway with a piercing scream. "Ahhhhhhh."

Aaron was caught off guard when Corey lunged at him but managed to catch sight of the crowbar bearing down toward his head. At the last second, Aaron shifted his body to the left and felt the bones on his right collarbone snap like twigs on a branch. Pain seared through his body, and he shrieked out in anguish. He dropped the knife, which skidded under the chair, and grabbed his shoulder.

Corey raised his arms high into the air and came down with the crowbar again, but Aaron dodged it this time. Corey continued his assault and swung the weapon like a baseball bat, striking Aaron in his thigh, forcing him to his knees. When Corey raised the weapon again, Aaron grabbed Corey's foot and lifted it in the air, knocking Corey off balance and into the wooden chair. Isabella's mom fell onto the floor, and the crowbar dropped from Corey's hands.

Aaron stood up with his arm sagging by his side and most of his weight on his uninjured leg. He shuffled past Corey towards the crowbar by the stairs. Corey reached up for Aaron's foot with both of his hands and wrapped his arms around Aaron's ankle, preventing him from moving. Aaron curled his hand into a fist and punched Corey in the side of the head. Corey's eyes glazed over, and he blinked several times but maintained his firm grip on Aaron's ankle. Aaron punched Corey again, this time in the ribs, forcing Corey to let go of his grip.

Aaron bent down to pick up the crowbar when he was overcome by excruciating pain throughout his body. He put his hand to his lower back, and warm wetness seeped through his fingers. He turned and saw Isabella standing behind him with the bloody knife in her hand. Aaron staggered back into the wall, and then gravity took over. He slid down the yellow striped wallpaper leaving a trail of blood in his wake.

Isabella dropped the knife and ran to her mother lying on the floor. She peeled the duct tape from her mother's lips and gently placed her mother's head on her lap. With tears falling from her eyes, Isabella brushed her mother's hair back from her face.

"Oh, Mom. I'm so sorry. I'm so sorry," Isabella sniffled.

Corey crawled over to Isabella and put his hand on her shoulder.

Isabella heard a faint moan, but it wasn't coming from her mother. She looked in Aaron's direction, but he was gone.

"Corey! Where is he?" Isabella held her mother like a lioness protecting her cub.

Corey stood up, his hand covering his ribs, and stumbled towards the stairs. A trail of blood was smeared across the wooden floor into the dining room.

Corey looked back at Isabella. "Behind you!"

Isabella turned, and out of the corner of her eye, she saw Aaron charging at her. She shifted her body up against the wall, dropping her mother to the floor. The crowbar whistled above her head and hit the wall behind her, showering pieces of drywall into her hair. She crab-walked back down the hallway towards the front door.

Aaron yanked the crowbar from the wall and raised it above his head. He lifted his leg over Mrs. McCormick's limp, frail body towards Isabella, and just before he could place his foot on the ground, Isabella's mother reached up and grabbed Aaron's foot, knocking him off balance. Aaron tumbled down with so much momentum that he didn't have time to brace himself. His head hit the leg of the chair, snapping it off, and he rolled onto his back, screaming as blood poured from his eye down the side of his face and onto the floor. He covered his eye with his hands, trying to stop the flow of blood.

Corey ran over to Isabella and picked her up off the floor. They held each other and watched Aaron flop around like a fish on a dock, trying desperately to get back into the water. The side of Aaron's head hit the coffee table with so much force that it knocked the glass of water over. The liquid crept to the edge of the table and fell in a steady stream into Aaron's open mouth. The glass rolled off the table, hit the wooden floor, and shattered into pieces next to his face. Small shards of crystal lodged into the side of his neck and cheek.

Corey and Isabella braced themselves for the possibility of yet another gruesome death – *if* the water was contaminated. They would not turn away this time.

Lying in a pool of blood and water, Aaron made a gurgling coughing sound, and it was evident that he was choking on the blood filling the back of his mouth. He grabbed his throat with both hands and shook his head side to side as he convulsed and spewed white foam like a rabid dog. All at once, Aaron's body straightened, and his hands moved from his throat to the sides of his body, with his thumbs pointing at his thighs.

As a sense of relief washed over Corey and Isabella, something unexpected occurred.

Aaron sat up!

Pink foam jetted from his mouth, and his eyelids popped open, revealing a film of blood concealing his pupils and irises. Red liquid flowed from his nostrils and gushed from the inside corners of his eyes. The upper half of Aaron's body snapped back toward the floor, and his skull slammed into the wood so hard, you could hear a crack.

Corey and Isabella stayed alert this time, half expecting something else to happen. When Aaron's body didn't move, Isabella hurried over to her mother, lying on the hallway floor.

"Mom? Can you hear me?"

Corey joined Isabella on the floor and took one of her mother's hands.

"Isabella…don't….drink the water," her mother said with her eyes closed.

"I won't, Mom. I won't." Isabella reached down and covered her mother's bloody hand with her own. "I love you, Mom."

"Your father…" Her mother coughed up blood onto her chest. "…would be so proud of you."

Isabella squeezed her mother's hand tighter and had difficulty speaking. "Yes…he would."

"I love you. Tell Corey…." Her mother's voice trailed off, and her head sank in Isabella's lap. The rise and fall of her chest ceased while her hand released its grip from Isabella's and dropped to the floor.

Isabella rested her head on her mother's chest and sobbed uncontrollably. She cradled her arms around her mother's limp body and tried to sing the song that her mother had sung to her when she was a little girl, but she couldn't get the words out.

With tears in his eyes, Corey put his arm around Isabella and held her as she mourned her mother's passing.

A sliver of sun stretched across the front lawn and through the screen porch door. Blades of grass, dipped in morning dew, glistened like diamonds. The rooster crowd his morning alarm, and the animals in the barn stirred.

Corey held Isabella as she fell into an exhausted asleep, embracing her mother.

CHAPTER 17

The day was bright, and the sky was clear, as the warm sun poured through the screen porch door into the hallway. In the corner, just before the kitchen entrance, stood a table garnished with fresh cut flowers, and above it, hanging on the wall, was a portrait of Isabella's parents, which had been painted by Isabella.

"Are you ready?" Corey called up from the bottom of the stairs.

"Almost. I'll be right down," Isabella replied.

Corey wandered into the living room to turn off the television when he saw a female reporter on the screen. She was in the downtown area of the city, and behind her, lining the streets, were vans from other television networks. She spoke with a kind, soft voice.

"A year ago today, a biochemical attack on our city left thousands dead and hundreds more with life-altering injuries. Men, women, and children have endured pain and suffering in their grieving process. Some may never recover from the loss of a loved one." The reporter looked away from the camera, wiped her eyes, and then continued. "This tragedy will be remembered forever, and we're here to honor those who died on that fateful day and remember the ones who lived. It will take a long time for this city to get back to normalcy, and we get stronger each day."

The reporter turned her head toward city hall and then back to the camera, "The mayor is about to address the city and reveal a monument in honor of the fallen victims."

Corey took the remote control from the living room table and turned the television off. He started up the stairs to check on Isabella when he caught sight of her standing on the top step. Her hair had been pulled to one side, allowing it to cascade over her shoulder. Her light blue dress made her hazel eyes sparkle.

Isabella held on to the handrail, descended the stairs, and when she reached the bottom step, Corey took her hand and pressed his lips to the back of it.

"You're just as beautiful now as when I first met you in France," Corey said.

"Thank you," Isabella replied blushing.

Isabella put her arm in the crux of Corey's elbow, and they walked onto the front porch together. Corey closed the screen door behind him, making sure not to let it slam into the wooden frame.

Isabella smiled. "Mom would have liked that."

They took the wooden stairs down to the gravel driveway, crossed the manicured lawn, and headed to the back of the house. Isabella stopped and picked some Black-eyed Susans from a small flower garden her mother had planted many years ago. She gazed off in the distance and then looked back at Corey, her eyes brimming with tears.

"I'm so proud of you." Corey kissed Isabella's forehead.

They continued arm in arm across the lush green grass. The sun warmed their faces, and a light breeze swirled through Isabella's hair. Horses galloped in the fields, chickens clucked and bobbed their heads around the property, and pigs rolled in mud, snorting in delight. The rotation of the windmill blades *whooshed* as it pushed clean water along the trench.

Corey and Isabella had arrived at their destination. They kneeled side by side, and Isabella laid the flowers across the ground.

"Hi, Mom. Hi, Dad," Isabella announced.

Two ornately carved granite gravestones rose from the ground in front of Corey and Isabella. Her mother's mauve-colored headstone was carved in an intricate display of flowers, symbolizing her beauty and patience. Her father's headstone was light gray, with a carving of the farm's windmill in the center of it, symbolizing his strength of character and resilience. At the bottom of both headstones was a carving of an outstretched hand as if the souls of Isabella's parents were reaching out for one another for eternity. On each stone, below their respective pictures, date of birth, and passing, was one sentence.

A woman admired by all and truly loved by one man

A man respected by all and truly loved by one woman

Corey admired Isabella's parents' dedication and love for each other and hoped that he and Isabella would always have that same kind of love.

Isabella wiped the tears from her eyes. "I miss you both so much. I will never be able to thank you for how you raised me and what you did to protect me. I will always be grateful to you. I love you!"

Isabella stood up and brushed off the grass from the front of her dress, while Corey remained kneeling. She looked down at him. "Are you ok?"

Corey adjusted his position from kneeling on both knees to kneeling on one knee. He turned, faced Isabella, and reached into his pants pocket.

"I wanted to do this in front of your parents, hoping they would give me their blessing. I never got the chance to meet your father, but I know what an amazing man he was from the stories you've shared with me," Corey lamented.

Isabella stood still with her hands raised to her mouth and her hazel eyes sparkling.

"Your mom was a remarkable woman. She treated me like I was her son, and I will never forget that. She treasured you. She gave her life for you. That is something I will always be indebted to her for." Corey paused. His heart was beating in his throat.

"Isabella, will you marry me?"

Isabella turned her eyes toward her parents' graves as if asking for their approval and then brought her eyes back to Corey.

"Yes! Yes! Yes!"

Corey slid the ring on her finger, stood up, wrapped his arms around Isabella, and kissed her. The world was silent for that brief moment as they clung together. Their memories of the past and their hopes for the future blended into the quiet joy of the present.

Corey and Isabella strolled across the grass, holding hands, ready to begin their new life together.

CPSIA information can be obtained
at www.ICGtesting.com
Printed in the USA
BVHW041923070221
599596BV00029B/419

9 781637 323755